MW00585347

ARACHNOPHOBIA

K. LUCAS

SHADOW PRESS

YOUR WORST FEAR REALIZED

ARACHNO PHOBIA

K. LUCAS

Copyright © 2022 by K. Lucas

All rights reserved.

No part of this book may be reproduced in any form or by any electronic or mechanical means, including information storage and retrieval systems, without written permission from the author, except for the use of brief quotations in a book review.

This is a work of fiction. All the names, characters, businesses, places, events and incidents in this book are either the product of the author's imagination or used in a fictitious manner. Any resemblance to actual persons, living or dead, or actual events is purely coincidental.

EBook ISBN: 978-1-958445-10-5

Paperback ISBN: 978-1-958445-12-9

Hardback ISBN: 978-1-958445-11-2

Cover Design by Pretty In Ink Creations

Editing and Proofreading by My Brother's Editor

For my son

PART I

Asia stood staring up at the opening carved into the side of the cliff. Jagged edges of stone jutted out above an expanse of black, making the entrance look like a sinister open mouth, with the words: *Warning: Do Not Enter* carved into an old wooden sign blocking the way. She looked back toward Cody and the others who were busy rolling their joints.

"Hey, are you sure we should go in there? It doesn't really look safe."

"Don't be such a pussy," one of Cody's buddies called back.

Cody elbowed him in the side.

"Hey, watch it, man!" his friend cried. "You'll make me spill. This shit is medical grade!"

Cody gave him and the others who were snickering a dark look. To Asia, he said, "It's safe, babe, don't worry. They just put the sign there for tourists. Besides, once you're in there, you won't want to miss it. Trust me."

Their confidence didn't make her feel much better. Asia knew well that there was one thing these stoners felt when they got high, and it was confidence—no matter how stupid the situation they found themselves in. She wanted to ask more questions, wanted to insist they go back to town to get some safety gear or at least some more layers of clothing. It was freezing outside and looked like it would be even colder in there.

Asia pictured being deep down in the depths of the cave, shivering in the dark, while her boyfriend's buddies laughed at her for being cold. *Forget the temperature, watch us all get our heads caved in from falling rocks, or I'll be the one to slip and break an ankle while the others are too high to even be able to help me up.* Her mind went in circles, imagining tragedy befalling their group while they were all too baked to help themselves.

She started to speak, but when she saw the looks on Cody's friends' faces, she let it drop. *They already hate me. Why give them another reason?* Asia was fully aware they wanted Cody to dump her, had been nudging him to do it since before graduation. She was here to impress them so they would grow to like her. She wanted to show them she was fun, wasn't a coward or a stick in the mud. She could be one of them if they'd just let her.

Against her better judgment, Asia pushed her concern aside. She asked, "You done with those yet?" motioning toward the wrapped marijuana.

Cody grinned at her before licking the edge of the wrap closed and passing her the joint. "Be my guest," he said.

Her face flamed as the others watched her ignite

the lighter and take the first inhale. She breathed in deep, feeling the burn far down in her lungs, but held it for a few moments before pushing out a solid plume of white smoke—nearly hacking up her lungs in the process. When she was done, she passed the joint back to Cody with a kiss.

The others gave her approving looks before lighting and sharing their own.

Once everyone had had a few hits and was nice and high, the group moved toward the cave's entrance.

ASIA'S PUPILS grew as the THC flooded her system. The worry lines on her forehead eased as her entire face relaxed. Cody pulled her close, wrapping one strong arm around her waist and holding her next to him as they approached the cave.

She leaned on him, letting him support her as they walked. Smoking hit Asia harder than Cody and his friends because she wasn't as used to it as they were. She tried to hide the effect it had on her, but Cody wasn't fooled. He stopped, letting the others get a ways ahead, then pulled her even closer to kiss her.

"Come on, you guys," one of the others called. "At least wait until we're inside before you do that shit."

"That's disgusting," another cried.

Asia turned scarlet. *Hypocrites,* she thought. Cody only laughed beside her before grabbing her hand and nudging her along the rest of the way to the entrance.

As soon as they entered, they turned on their flash-lights. Asia realized the cheap lights they had didn't do much to shine their way in this darkness. *We should've stopped to get headlamps,* she thought.

"How did you hear about this place again?" she asked Cody, fear dripping from every word.

"We're only an hour from home. Lots of us have heard stories about it," one of the others said.

They continued farther into the cave, Cody failing to notice Asia's shivering growing more violent with each passing minute. At one point, he tripped, holding on to the wall for support to keep from going all the way down. A slimy, gooey substance, almost like snot, was on his hand and between his fingers. "Gross!" he said, wiping it on his jeans.

"Oh my god, Cody! Get that away from me!" Asia shrieked. Her voice echoed slightly, traveling around them and back toward the entrance. She took a few steps back when she felt a spider web across her face and hair. She cried out even louder, swinging her arms in a desperate attempt to get away from the web.

"Keep it down," one of the others said. "You don't wanna bring bats down on us, do you?"

"B-bats?" Asia cried, slightly quieter.

"No, there're no bats," Cody said, annoyed with his friends. He moved to help Asia with the invisible web. Then he looked to the others. "Come on, guys, stop messing with Asia. We're almost there."

A few more minutes of walking, then they spilled out into an open chamber. Asia gasped, "Oh, it's beautiful."

They stared out at the enormous area, filled with

different types of rocks and marble of all shapes and sizes. The flashlights shone over the rocks, and she felt more than ever that the cave seemed like the giant mouth of a beast waiting to swallow them whole.

A shudder racked through Asia when Cody pulled her to him again.

"Okay, we'll be over here," one of his friends said, irritated again. "I don't know about you, but I need another hit." The rest of them moved across the area to a group of boulders that were the perfect size for the group to sit on.

I hope there're no more spider webs, Asia thought as Cody led her away into a more private area. She didn't think she'd be able to see them first, would only know when she was caught in one again, and the thought of having to feel that on her hair and skin, or screaming in there again, made her queasy.

"Come on," he whispered. "They won't see us over here."

Asia followed wordlessly until he found the place he wanted. He pulled her through a narrow opening between two enormous boulders, and again Asia thought she felt a spider web across her face and hair. She shrieked—an automatic reaction, feeling the prickling sensation across her entire skull.

She jumped back from Cody, scratching at her hair and scalp, flipping her hair over, and shaking it to get the spider and its web out. "Get it off, get it off!" she wailed, almost in tears now.

Cody held still, wincing at the sound of her screams. He started to reach a hand toward her, not sure what he'd be able to do to help with all her flailing, when she smacked him in her desperate attempts. He pulled back.

"Do you see anything?" she said. "Shine your light on me!"

Cody did as she asked, looking closely for any sign of a web or spider. "You got it," he said. "It's gone."

Asia breathed.

"Come on, let's go. And try not to yell. I don't know how stable those rocks are." He pointed up to the jagged spear-like rocks wedged into the roof of the cavern.

"I'm sorry. I couldn't help it."

"I know." Cody took her hand, leading her the rest of the way to the spot he had in mind. When they were situated, Asia sat in awe of the cavern's beauty as Cody slowly ran a hand up her thigh.

There came a loud rumbling noise, and the ground began to quake beneath their feet. Asia screamed again, this time even louder. They heard the screams of the others not far away. Cody gritted his teeth and was about to yell out too, but then it stopped.

Everything was quiet and still once more.

"What the hell was that?" Asia whispered, tears streaming. Her high was gone, and she no longer cared about impressing anyone. What she cared about now was getting the hell out of the cave in one piece, without any rocks smashing her brains in.

She stood, ready to move back the way they'd come. Some of the rocks had shifted, making the way back through the narrow boulders a little too narrow. She started to push, growing frantic when they wouldn't budge. *We're trapped. Oh my god, we're going to die in here, we're never getting out, we're going to starve, to fucking DIE in here!*

Her fingernails scratched along the surface of the rock so hard, so frenzied, that two of them peeled back, dangling from her fingers by part of the cuticle. As Asia howled in pain, clutching her injured hand, bleeding against her body, Cody moved to help push against the rock.

"It's okay, Asia. We'll get out of here," he said, trying to convince himself as much as her. He pushed but couldn't get the rock to move any more than she could. "Guys! A little help over here!" he called to the others.

"Help us!" Asia screamed.

Cody winced at the high-pitched wail. He knew she was being too loud in here, her voice causing too much echo. He stopped pushing to grab on to Asia and pull her back into his arms. He rubbed her back, trying to soothe her, trying to urge her to calm down. "Hey," he whispered. "We have to be quieter, remember?"

"I can't," she cried. "I can't die in here, Cody."

"We're not going to. We're going to be fine. It was just a little earthquake or something—no big deal. We're fine."

"Why aren't the others answering us?"

Cody listened, sure he would hear someone calling back to them. He waited.

Nothing.

"They might be stuck too."

"Oh my god, oh my god, what are we going to do?" Asia ran her hands through her hair, starting to yank at her roots. When she stepped into the beam of the flashlight, Cody could see the blood from her hurt fingers running into her hair.

"Listen," Cody hissed. He could've sworn—there! There it was again. Asia wouldn't stop. He grabbed her arm to get her to hear what he was trying to say. "Listen, there's something—"

Asia stopped. She heard it too—some kind of movement in the cavern. "What—"

"Shh! I dunno." He held up his hand for her to wait.

They both strained to hear what was making the movement and where it was coming from. It seemed like every noise echoed all around and it was hard to pinpoint anything. They both held their breath, waiting for the noise to grow louder.

2

It sounded like something scuttling its way through the dark—a small creature bounding over the tops of loose rocks. Asia gripped Cody's arm tight, staring wide eyed into the cavern's void.

"Cody," she whispered.

It was too quiet. The others weren't making any noises, still hadn't responded to their calls for help. Something was wrong here. They both felt it.

"It's getting closer," Cody whispered back.

"Should we—"

A high-pitched screech broke the silence, followed by the sounds of Cody's friends all crying out at once in a frenzied plea for help. "Hey!" Cody screamed. "We're over here! What's going on!"

Asia heard the sound of rocks falling nearby, wincing in hope that they wouldn't fall near where she and Cody stood. She and Cody renewed their efforts to push against the boulders. One finally started to budge.

They pushed harder, shifting it slowly until, finally, there was room to squeeze through.

Cody shined the flashlight through the opening, making sure the way was completely clear. "Looks good, you go first," he said.

SHE WENT. But as he started to follow, he found that although the gap was wide enough for Asia, it wasn't for him.

The others were still screaming incoherent cries for help. *What the hell is happening over there?* Cody thought as he tried to shove his way through. He sucked in his gut, which only made his chest push out. Nothing he did was enough to squeeze his broad body through the narrow opening.

ASIA TURNED BACK with the absence of the flashlight, realizing Cody wasn't behind her. "Cody? What's wrong?"

"I'm stuck. I can't fit through."

She started to go back for him—then she felt something move her hair. Asia jerked back in surprise, raising her hurt hand to run through her hair. *Fucking spiderwebs!* she thought, trying not to scream again.

She weaved her fingers through her hair, making sure—she stopped. Something *was* in her hair! Something was *crawling* through her hair! No longer able to hold back her scream, she released a guttural cry that traveled clear to the outside of the cave.

"Fuck! What's wrong?" Cody called, doubling his efforts to get through to her.

Asia didn't answer. She couldn't. She was whipping her head back and forth, flinging her long hair in a frantic flurry, more panicked now than ever. Her hands held fistfuls of her hair, shaking and throwing, shaking and throwing, over and over again.

Whatever was in her hair was going to build a nest, was going to travel down into her earlobe at night—lay eggs in her brain! She had to get it off of her, out of her hair. *If I make it out of here, I swear I'm shaving it all off!*

Asia's spine tingled with awareness. She felt a thousand little legs crawling all over her body, through every strand of her hair, across every pore of her skin. The tiny hairs on the back of her neck stood to attention.

Something touched her upper arm. Asia screamed again, lashing out blindly.

"Hey, it's me. It's okay."

She stopped, panting, wiping the tears from her blurry vision. She realized she was back by Cody again, saw how he was wedged in close, unable to pass through the enormous boulders. They wrapped their arms around each other, Asia sobbing into him. "I'm sorry. There was something in my hair. I hate spiders so much!"

As Cody held her, it dawned on him how silent the cave was again. "The others stopped yelling," he said.

"Do you think they left without us?"

"No... they wouldn't do that," he said, not really sure

anymore what they would do. "They probably went to get help or maybe they're just saving their voices so they don't get thirsty."

Asia wouldn't put it past them at all to leave if they got the chance. This place was giving her the creeps with all the strange noises and cobwebs everywhere, and now the earthquake or whatever it was. They liked to act tough, but Cody's friends would get the hell out of Dodge the first chance they got.

"Shine the light up," she said, thinking maybe they could somehow climb up and out—maybe she could give him a boost or something.

Cody swiveled the flashlight up. He stumbled back, his jaw falling open, almost dropping the light. "No w—"

His cry was cut off as a giant spider, nearly the size he was, lunged forward. Its fangs drove down deep into his chest with a swift jab. The flashlight dropped, fading to a dim flicker on the floor. Cody blinked, feeling the venom branch out along his veins. *This isn't happening. I'm still high. They laced my weed with something and I'm hallucinating—*

Asia was a deer frozen in the headlights, numb, paralyzed, incapable of thought. Eight coal-black eyes stared back at her through the darkness as she watched Cody's body twitch and convulse. The spider reached back its two front legs, then began to spin a web around Cody's body.

Asia broke out in a cold sweat. *It's going to eat him,* she thought. Then it finally registered. *I'm next. It's going to come after me next.* She wanted to scream again, to cry out louder than ever, to wail against this beast, this goddamned *bug!*

As the spider spun Cody's body into a web, Asia slowly inched her way back through the crevice that was too small for him to fit. The flashlight went out, leaving her in total darkness. She took a step backward and then another until she was far enough away to spin around and run.

The movement caught the spider's attention. It dropped Cody, emitting a hiss that made Asia's blood curdle. She ran faster, hearing the spider scurrying above her. One of its long, hairy legs reached down in front of her, but like Cody, the spider was too large to fit inside the crevice now that the rocks had fallen.

The spider hissed again before pulling back. Asia looked up, but it was too dark to see anything. She kept going, back into the large open cavern. Cody's friends were in heaps on the other side, spider's webs glistening off their bodies. *I'm glad it's too dark in here. I'm glad I can't see them better,* she thought, knowing that if she did see them, she would probably lose her sanity.

She tripped, caught herself, then fell hard. As she landed, her jaw slammed shut, making her bite her own tongue. Asia's eyes watered from the pain. She tasted the blood pooling in her mouth, wanting to stay down, to roll up in a little ball on her side, cry, and wait to be saved.

The sounds coming from all around her told her she couldn't do that, no matter how badly she wanted to. *I'm not going to be eaten by a fucking spider!* Just as she had the thought, she felt something crawling on her hand. Invisible little legs creeping along her skin, between her fingers, up her arm.

Asia brushed herself off, waving her hands around, trying to get the creature or creatures off of her. It took all the strength she possessed to not scream again, to not draw the monster to her. She got back to her feet, spit the blood from her mouth, and kept going.

It was getting closer. Asia could feel it behind her, creeping through the rocks, slinking up the sides of the cave. She spun behind her but could see nothing in the blackness. She faced forward, stumbling again but not falling. *Almost there!* she told herself, begging for it to be true.

Then—there it was. The glowing light of the cave entrance, dim in the fading light of the day. As weak as the light was, it was bright enough for Asia to see what she wished she couldn't.

Hundreds of tiny black spiders were crawling all over the floor of the cave, across the roof, and down the walls—coming for her. She was surrounded. And behind them all—was the mammoth staring at her with those eight black eyes, darker than the deepest depths of the cave. As scary as the tiny ones were, they were nothing compared to the giant one.

Asia ran for the opening. She heard them—felt them crunch and squish open beneath her shoes, heard their hissing, their terrible little feet moving over the stone, saw them swarm her like she was a meal about to get away. *That's exactly what I am to them.*

Then Asia noticed something else. All the spiders, no matter the size, were shrinking from the light. As she drew nearer to the entrance, they fell back into the shadows, still following but doing anything to keep out of the beam of light.

With a sliver of hope, she pushed herself harder. She was almost to the entrance now—just a few more feet. The mammoth was almost on top of her now, hissing at her like a feral cat. It reached one of its enormous legs toward her, but Asia was fully in the light now. The spider shrieked, tucked its leg back into itself, and scurried away.

She turned to watch it go—a knee-jerk reaction—when she fell again. Her chin and the side of her face skinned against the cold stone floor. There was a sickening pop as her knee came into contact with a rock, and she finally released the scream she'd been holding back as the little black spiders swarmed her legs that were now back out of the light.

They drove their fangs down into her, biting and clawing, spinning webs furiously, crawling all over her jeans and down into her shoes. Asia panicked. The pain was like nothing she'd experienced in her life. The sensation of the *things* on her nearly made her lose control of her bladder. They were on her legs and feet, but she felt they were everywhere else too—in her hair, on her face, crawling up her shirt, looking for any way to gain access *inside*.

She stood, stumbled, then pushed past the pain and ran—five more feet, then outside into the blessed light. Asia screamed and screamed until her throat was raw, then she screamed some more, all the while still running, never looking back at the cave. She felt the spiders falling off of her in droves, shrinking back to the forest floor, some almost seemed to be *melting*. She peeled her clothes off, not caring that she was naked, only wanting to get every piece of them off her body until she could no longer feel the *legs*.

Asia came to the cars parked a ways down the hill— and realized she didn't have the keys. *Cody* had them. "Fuck!" she screamed, slamming a fist against the car window. She looked up at the sky filled with clouds, saw the sun going down, and knew she had to get as far away from this place as she could.

Asia turned in the direction that held the most sunlight, then set off on foot.

PART II

3

"I need to take a shit!" Hart yelled across the travel trailer.

"*Again*?" Ivey said. "Honey, this is getting really old. You just got home from work and it's been twice already."

"I'm sorry. Look, do you need to go? This is coming in about a minute."

Ivey sighed, defeated. Hart refused to take medication for his IBS, refused to see a doctor. It seemed like every time he ate, he had to blow up the bathroom within five minutes. She might not mind so much if their family of four wasn't sharing a single bathroom in an RV of less than three hundred square feet.

"Kids, go pee if you need to. Dad has to poop again!" she called. She looked at her husband. "I can't take much more of this, Hart."

He had to go so bad he was hopping up and down like a little kid about to wet himself. He nodded to her. "I know. I'm sorry." Neither of the kids answered, so he moved to do his business. The bathroom vent fan turned on with a squeak and a groan, warning the family that they might want to get outside for a while.

Ivey went to the bunkhouse where the kids were each on their iPads. "Come on, guys, we better get some fresh air for a bit."

Xander came without complaint, leaving his tablet on his bed and hopping down from the top bunk.

Kala groaned, "God, Dad is so gross!"

"Don't say that, you know he has a condition."

"It's still gross!"

"He's going to see a doctor soon."

Kala rolled her eyes, giving her mom a look that said *I've heard that one before.*

Ivey herded them out the door, thinking, *we need to check with the county on Monday. How long has it been since we applied for that building permit? Over six months now?* She tried to do the math in her head, but it was too hard to calculate.

Living on the land they'd bought, while they built a house, had been Hart's brilliant idea. She tried not to hold the strain their family was going through against him. It wasn't his fault the county was taking so long. *No, but it is his fault the RV stinks half the time*, she thought. *I don't know what I'll do when it's winter break from school.*

"Mom, look at that huge moth!" Xander cried, pointing at a moth hanging in the shade of a nearby tree branch. He held his hands out, seeing that the moth was bigger than both his hands put together. "Wow!" he cried.

"What is it with you and gross things?" Kala said, moving farther away from him.

"Kala!" Ivey cried.

"What? It's true. He's always poking at creepy-crawly things. It's disgusting, just like Dad."

"Moths aren't creepy-crawly," Xander said.

"You know what I mean." Kala gave him one of her infamous eye rolls before finding a seat farther down the driveway.

"I'm sorry, honey. You know she's in a mood. This situation is hard on all of us, especially on weekends when we're all home," Ivey said.

"I wish it wasn't Friday. I wish the weekend would never come."

Ivey pulled him in close to hold. "I'm sorry," she said again.

"How much longer is it gonna be?" Xander asked, trying not to cry.

"We'll check in with the county again on Monday, okay? It should be any day now."

He only nodded before moving off toward the trees.

"Don't go far, okay?" Ivey called.

Xander waved a hand at her.

She plopped down in a fold-up chair beneath the awning, unable to keep from hearing the sounds coming from the bathroom. Ivey put her head into her hands and started to cry.

LATER IN THE EVENING, there was another fight about what was for dinner. Xander wanted to order pizza, but Kala was tired of it—they'd just had it last week.

"I'll just throw some chicken on," Ivey said, heading toward the fridge to get the supplies.

"Not chicken *again*," Hart said, sounding almost just like Kala.

"Yeah, I'm tired of chicken," Xander agreed.

"Alright, tacos then," Ivey said.

All three of them groaned at that.

I should just make some for myself and let the three of them fend for themselves! Ivey was fed up with the arguing, irritated that nobody liked her cooking no matter what she made, even if it wasn't chicken or tacos.

"Mom, we need to just order from a restaurant. We can have it delivered, no big deal," Kala said, sounding as if she'd solved the world's biggest problem with the snap of her fingers.

"They don't deliver out here, remember?"

"What? No way. They have to."

"We're in the middle of nowhere, dear."

"Town isn't that far."

"Twenty minutes down a highway is a bit far for delivery. And there aren't exactly a lot of choices in town as far as restaurants go," Hart said.

Kala stared at him, then at her mom. Tears pooled in her eyes. "You did this!" she cried before standing and storming into the bunkhouse, slamming the door behind her.

Hart hung his head, knowing that his family resented him.

Ivey placed a hand on his arm, kissing his cheek. "I'll make some sandwiches," she said.

As THEY ATE, Kala snuck out of the bunkhouse into the bathroom. *Better take a shower before Dad blows it up in here again*, she thought. The worst was at night when everyone was in bed.

Whatever he did in the RV past dark, they all suffered because they couldn't get out of bed and stay outside for an hour in the middle of the night. The smell would linger for hours unless they opened the windows, and with winter fast approaching, they couldn't do that without freezing. *Freeze or suffocate,* she thought.

Kala saw that it was growing dark outside now, even though it was barely five o'clock. It wouldn't be long before her dad finished dinner and had to do his business *again*. Better to take a shower early and not have to deal with it.

Preparing herself to take one of the shortest showers of her life—all of them in the RV had to be short because they only had so much hot water—Kala stepped into the tiny shower, forced to turn sideways in order to fit. She reached for the handle, turned, and when no water came out, slammed a fist against the shower wall. *I hate my life!* she thought.

"Will you turn on the pump!" she screamed louder than necessary. The others were just on the other side of the wall—they'd hear even if she didn't yell at all, but it felt good to scream so she kept doing it until she finally heard the sound of the water pump turn on.

Water flowed through the showerhead. Kala rinsed before shutting it off again to save water while she soaped up, shivering against the cold air before she could turn the water back on and rinse once more. She allowed herself a moment of luxury to bask in the warm water while she washed the soap from her hair. As she did, she stared up at the darkening sky through the vent screen directly overhead.

Full moon tonight. Bogeyman might come out to play. Wouldn't that liven things up around here? She was about to turn back around to shut the water off again when she noticed a small black spider crawling on top of the vent screen. *Is that a black widow?* she wondered. Then she realized it couldn't be because it was too small.

This one was so small it could almost squeeze through one of the square holes in the screen. *You're never going to fit through there,* she thought, then immediately thought she might be wrong about that. Her eyes traveled across the screen to the spot where a couple of the holes looked old and worn. Kala was transfixed, watching the tiny spider try to squeeze its way through until the water began to run cold.

She gasped, reaching to twist it off as it turned nearly to ice on her back. When Kala looked back up at the vent, the spider was gone. Her head prickled with the sensation of little legs moving through her hair. She ran a hand over her wet hair to make sure it wasn't on her, shuddering.

"You okay in there?" her dad called from the other

side of the wall. "You didn't get sucked down the drain, did you?"

Kala realized she'd been standing there staring again, she hadn't even been able to condition her hair or shave yet. "Waiting for the water to heat up," she called back. Her stomach rumbled at the sound of her family eating dinner without her. *They never care when I'm gone. It's just business as usual*, she thought.

As she stood shivering, waiting for the water heater to warm a few more gallons of water, she considered if she wanted to bother shaving or not. She was too cold, too hungry, too *annoyed* to care about having hairy legs today. Deciding to get it over with—she was sure her dad would have to shit again any minute—Kala smoothed some conditioner over her hair, braced for the cold water, then finished with her shower.

She didn't see the tiny little eyes watching her from above, considering how they might find a way down through the screen.

4

Ivey stood to collect the paper plates and put dinner away. From the corner of her eye, she saw Hart eyeing the bathroom door, growing impatient for Kala to finish with her shower. She watched Xander get up from the table to move into the bunkhouse where his iPad was waiting for him to pick it back up.

"You about done in there?" Hart groaned, looking like he wanted to knock the bathroom door down just to get to the toilet.

"Did the sandwiches make you sick?" Ivey asked.

"I think it was the chips," he said, beads of sweat already forming on his forehead.

"Honey, you have got to do something about this."

"I *know*, okay? I know."

The sound of Xander's game drifted to Ivey. She listened for Kala but realized she wasn't making any sounds in the bathroom—no water pump, no shuffling around, no bumping into the door like everyone always did because it was so small in there. She moved to knock on the door. "Kala? Everything okay?"

"Can I get five minutes to myself?" Kala snapped back.

Ivey held her hands up in mock surrender, met Hart's eyes, and gave him a look that said, *I'm staying out of it.* She took three steps back into the kitchen area to finish putting the food away. *The permit application probably still hasn't even been reviewed*, she thought, disgusted again with how long this process was taking, with what it was doing to her family.

They were all a bunch of grouches, could barely stand the sight of one another. Everything was annoying to everyone—especially Kala, who always had a complaint waiting at the tip of her tongue.

The bickering was nonstop when they were all home, even as they spent most of their time outside. Now that the weather was growing colder, it was getting harder to spend so much time outdoors. Winter was right around the corner and the chill was upon them, forcing them to spend more time than any of them liked inside.

Ivey hated to think what the kids at school said about Xander and Kala, hoping they didn't get picked on because of their temporary setup. *Kids can be so damned cruel*, she thought, trying not to picture her two getting teased. *Maybe nobody knows. Why would the kids need to know where we live anyway?* And just as she had the thought, she remembered what a small town they now lived in.

A pounding came at the door, pulling Ivey from her thoughts. She turned to Hart with wide eyes. "Who could that be?" she whispered.

Hart shrugged, too worried about his stomach to care about much else. "Go see," he said.

"I'm not opening that door! It's dark out."

"You want me to get it?"

The pounding came again, harder this time.

Ivey leaned forward across the counter to peek through the miniblinds. It was hard to get a clear view from her angle, but it looked like— "I think there's a girl out there, Hart."

"What?" He stood from the dinette, wincing, giving the bathroom door one more solid look. "Kala, you better hurry up. I'm not sure how much longer I can hold out." He stood next to Ivey and leaned forward to look through the slat she'd been peeking through.

"You see her?" Ivey whispered.

They watched together as the girl leaned forward into the trailer's outside light and pounded her fist against the side of the fiberglass. Ivey gasped. "She's *naked*!"

She and Hart shared another look, silently questioning what kind of shit just dropped on their front steps. They'd been married long enough for each to know what the other was considering without speaking a word. *This could be bad. This could be really, really bad.*

"What the hell?" Kala called from inside the bathroom.

"We can't just leave her out there," Ivey said to Hart, ignoring her daughter.

"You really want to bring her in here? With the kids? What if it's a trap?"

"I know! But god, Hart, what do we do? She looks Kala's age!"

Hart moved to the door, cracked it open, peeked out, still holding on to the door handle in case he needed to slam it back shut. "Hello?" he called.

"Please, do you have any more lights you can turn on?"

"Any more what?"

"Lights! Turn on the lights!"

Hart gave Ivey a look of pure confusion. "She wants me to turn on the lights," he said.

Ivey flipped on one of the kitchen lights. "Turn on the ones under the awning."

He reached for the switch.

"Please, do you have any more?" the girl outside cried.

Ivey watched through the window and could've sworn she saw something moving on the edge of the darkness. "Ask her if she needs help."

"Do you need any help?" Hart asked the girl, averting his eyes. The girl was around Kala's age, just like they'd first guessed, and she was indeed naked.

The girl was crying, mumbling something unintelligible to herself. Ivey strained to listen from behind Hart, but it was hard to make out anything clearly. She jumped as the bathroom door opened. Kala stepped out and, without warning, screamed at Xander, who was in his own world on his bed. "Get out! I need to get dressed!"

Ivey felt like she wanted to cry more now than ever. This girl needed help, but she had to look out for her own kids. They needed to call the police, but how could she tell a naked teenager to just stand out there in the dark until they showed up? She watched Kala with the towel wrapped around her, slipping into the bunkhouse as Xander moved to the couch.

If either of them were in a situation like this, I'd about die if they were forced to wait outside freezing, she thought. It was someone's daughter out there on her front steps. She was ashamed she'd even had to think about it.

The bunkhouse door slammed shut. Behind her, Hart said, "Hon, what do we do?" His tone was urgent.

Ivey realized he was more worried about pooping than anything else. She could see on his face that he didn't have the time to deal with this right now—had other more pressing matters to attend to.

"Where's your gun?" she asked.

"My *what?*"

"You're going to let that girl in here and then you're going to go take your shit. I'm going to defend my children, Hart, if shit hits the fan while you're in there, unable to do anything about it."

"You don't need the damned gun, Ivey," Hart hissed. He glanced back at the still cracked door, then gave Ivey a look as if to say, *she can hear every word we're saying!*

"I'm not taking any chances!" Ivey said, not giving a damn if the girl heard or not.

"Okay, okay." Hart opened the door a little wider. "Do you want to come in here?" he asked the girl.

Ivey cringed at how serial killer–like her husband sounded.

The girl had her back to the door now, standing almost directly beneath the RV lights. She was looking out into the dark that was growing darker by the minute, seeming to be scanning for something—or someone. It was as if she hadn't heard a word Hart said.

He stepped back. "I'll grab it," he said to Ivey as she took his place at the door.

She waited for him to get the gun, hand it to her, then take his place in the bathroom. The gun was heavy in her hand. Although it was cold, holding it made her palm sweat. It felt awkward and slippery— just holding it made her feel sick. *Girl, you better not do anything stupid. I really don't want to use this!* Ivey thought.

She looked around for a place to set it—somewhere it would be within reach if she needed it but also out of the way so she wouldn't have to hold it all night. *Perfect,* she thought when her eyes landed on the shelf above the TV.

Ivey set the gun down, then went back to the door. With a deep breath, she opened it all the way to see the girl shivering beneath the outside light. "Come inside," she said.

The girl looked back to Ivey, then swiveled around to look at the yard again. She couldn't keep her eyes in one place and to Ivey it was clear she was terrified of something out there. "You'll be safe inside," Ivey said.

The girl looked at her again. "You don't have to. I just need light."

"We have plenty of lights inside," Ivey promised. "Please, you're making me cold just looking at you."

The girl looked down at herself and then back to Ivey. "I'm sorry. I'm not a psycho, I promise."

Ivey smiled. "Come inside and tell me all about it."

The girl finally agreed. With one more look out into the night, she hurried up the RV steps, letting Ivey close and lock the door behind them.

5

I vey reached through the doorway to her and Hart's bedroom to pull one of the blankets from the bed. She folded it in half before wrapping it around the girl several times until she looked like she could barely move.

"We need to get out of here," the girl said.

Ivey shook her head. "Who can I call to come get you?"

"You don't understand. We all need to leave."

"We can't leave, honey. This is our land, our home. We have nowhere else to go."

The girl began to cry again. She looked around the RV, saw Xander on the couch, still in his own world, saw the bunkhouse and bathroom doors closed, saw all the shadows in the corners. "Please. We have to," she whispered.

Dread was worming its way down Ivey's spine. She didn't like the look in the girl's eyes or the pleading note in her tone. She was terrified of something alright and if the girl thought it would get them—Ivey needed to know exactly what the hell they were dealing with.

"Who's out there?" Ivey asked.

"No one—it's—you won't believe me!" the girl sobbed.

"I want to help you. I want to protect you and all of us." Ivey took the girl's hand and led her over to the dinette so she could sit down. "What's your name, honey?" she asked.

"Asia."

"Asia, please tell me what's going on. I don't care how unbelievable it sounds. I want to know."

Asia nodded. "Alright. But first—are there any more lights you can turn on?"

Ivey rose to flick on every light in the area. "Better?"

"Yes." Asia released a breath. "There are spiders out there. They came from a cave and they—" She choked back a sob. "They *ate* them!"

"Whoa!" Xander said, looking up from his tablet, now staring at the back of the girl's head.

Ivey shook her head at him. "Don't," she mouthed before he could say anything else. To Asia, she said, "Who... ate the spiders?"

Asia's eyes were saucers, tears streaming down her cheeks freely. She slowly shook her head. "The *spiders* ate *them*."

"Who'd they eat?"

"Cody and his friends. They're—they're all gone."

Ivey bit her lip, feeling the cold sweat break out on her forehead, just like Hart when he had to use the bathroom. "And these are... people?"

"Yes!" Asia cried. She leaned against the table, slamming her forehead down on top of it. "They're out there now," she said.

"The spiders?"

Asia lifted her head. "They're going to get in here. I know they followed me. I felt them the whole way, waiting for the sun to go all the way down, for me to step into the darkness."

"Why would they wait for that? Wouldn't they just come get you anyway?" Xander asked.

Ivey and Asia both turned to look at him. The tablet was completely out of his hands and locked now. He was utterly transfixed by Asia and her story.

"They don't like the light," Asia said. "They came from deep inside the cave where it doesn't exist."

"We better turn on some more lights," Xander said.

FROM THE OTHER side of the bathroom door, Hart sat on the toilet, pooping his guts out. He was on his phone, playing his favorite game while he had the chance, only halfway listening to the conversation going on a few feet away. He grimaced in pain as his gut gurgled, his bowels about to make another movement.

The fan buzzed overhead. It whined and squeaked loudly but not loudly enough to drown out the noises Hart made and did virtually nothing for the smell. Every few words he heard were drowned out by the sounds his body was making.

She's afraid of some spiders? You've got to be kidding me,

Hart thought. He heard his son chime into the conversation, listening to the talk about the dark and turning on the lights, then he thought, *This girl has really lost her marbles.*

His stomach cramping, Hart clamped down as he filled up the toilet with a mess of mushy half-diarrhea excrement. He scowled at himself, hating the pain, hating the smells, hating that this happened to him almost every time he ate.

Hart stood for a moment, twisting to step on the toilet's foot pedal. The toilet's inside flap opened, allowing the contents to drop down into the holding tank with a wet slap. He released the pedal and turned to sit back down, knowing it wouldn't be long before another burst ran through him.

He brought his game back up on his phone, tired of listening to all the talk about spiders, even more, tired of spending most of his spare time in the bathroom. As his character moved across the screen, he tapped frantically to defeat the villain and collect his reward. Just like his son on his iPad, Hart was soon lost in his own little world, oblivious to anything else going on around him.

Beneath him, the toilet's flap was still open a fraction of an inch—a wedge of feces blocking it from closing all the way. There wasn't enough room for his waste to slide through on its own, but there was just enough room for a few tiny black spiders to make their way up through the holding tank into the toilet bowl.

They scuttled around the sides of the bowl, avoiding the freshly falling poop as it dropped. A couple of the spiders were taken out by thick splashes of diarrhea, but there were still survivors. They made it all the way up to just under the rim of the toilet seat lid, where the flesh of Hart's posterior stuck through. From there, it was only a short way farther to their destination.

Damned ads, Hart thought, waiting for the *X* to appear so he could get out of the unwanted interruption of his game. Waiting for it to appear was like waiting for water to boil on the stove. There it was—he tapped the *X* before it disappeared and was once again immersed in his game, oblivious to what was happening in the bowl beneath him.

The tiny black spiders were gently crawling through his hairs—so softly he couldn't have felt them even if he was paying attention. They made their way all the way around to the entrance—or exit—of his body, and when he made his next purge, they made their entry.

A SCREAM CAME. Ivey, Asia, and Xander all stood, momentarily stunned. Kala screamed again—this time flying through the bunkhouse door, running to the couch and standing up on top of it. She pointed back toward the bedroom. "There's a spider!"

Asia paled. "We have to turn on more lights!" she cried.

Xander ran for the flashlights near the front door.

Ivey took a tentative step toward the bunkhouse. "What does it look like, Kala?"

"I don't know! It was black!"

"They're black and small," Asia said.

"That's the best you can tell me? How am I supposed to kill them?"

"All I know is they don't like light."

Ivey slipped her shoe off her foot and put it over her hand. She pounded against the bathroom door as she peeked into the bunkhouse. "You about done, Hart? Could really use your help!"

"I'm sick as a dog in here," came his muffled reply.

The kids watched with bated breath, none of them sure of what to do other than to keep the lights on. "Wait, take a flashlight," Xander called. He took one to Ivey, stepping back from her as she entered the room.

"We need to get out of here!" Asia warned again. "Please! It's not too late!"

Ivey ignored the girl, coming fully into her kids' bedroom. She shined the flashlight on the ceiling first, then the walls and floor. She couldn't see anything— "Where is it?" she called.

"In the corner!" Kala cried.

Ivey turned the light off, waiting to see if a spider would crawl out from the depths of darkness. Her eyes adjusted as she waited—nothing. "I don't—" There! She saw something—

She turned on the flashlight, beaming the light like a spotlight over a small black spider. She sighed, half-relieved, half-ashamed, that she was actually scared to death for a minute. "Found it! It's okay. It's just a daddy longlegs."

Leaving the lights on in the bunkhouse, she came back out to the couch where all three kids were waiting.

"It wasn't a daddy longlegs," Kala said. "I know what I saw."

"How do you know?" Xander asked.

She scowled at him. "I'm not lying."

"No one thinks that. Let's not argue, guys. We're all creeped out right now, okay?" Ivey said. She looked back to Asia who was chewing on her bottom lip to the point it was bleeding. Her hands were shaking at her sides, her eyes searching every square inch of the trailer.

The bathroom door rattled. The water pump came on. Then a moment later, Hart stepped out. "Whew, you guys do *not* want to go in there!" His grin fell when he saw the looks on everyone's faces. "What's eating everyone?"

6

A sia refused to go into the bunkhouse when Ivey offered to lend her some of Kala's clothes. "I'll just get dressed in the bathroom, if it's okay?" she said.

"Are you sure? It's so small in there…" Ivey said.

"There might be an after smell still," Hart said with a blush. It had been at least an hour since his visit in there, but he knew how the smell liked to linger.

"It's okay. I don't mind, really." Asia said. She looked like a rabbit caught in a trap, ready to bolt at any minute. When she looked at the bunkhouse—thought of going *inside*—her already pale face grew paler. She looked to Hart, pleading one last time. "We need to go. We need to get your family and get out of here while we still can."

Hart startled at the tears sliding down her cheek. He looked with questioning eyes to his wife who only shrugged. "We're safe here," he finally said. "I know it can seem a bit scary—like we're just in a fiberglass box

—but these walls are sturdy." He pounded his knuckles on the wall in an attempt to ease her mind. "Nothing is going to get us in here."

"*They* will," Asia said. "*It* will!"

"Why don't you come with me to pick something to wear," Ivey said.

Asia shook her head. "I'll wear whatever you choose."

"Thanks for asking me," Kala said under her breath.

"Kala, would you *please* pick something out for Asia to borrow?" Ivey said, eyebrows raised, eyes silently pleading for her daughter to cooperate.

Kala sulked into her room, picked her least favorite pajamas, then threw them at her mom before slamming her door and flopping on her bed.

Asia took the pajamas and headed into the bathroom.

ONLY NOW DID Asia dare look at her legs. She felt like she would die if she didn't scratch the itch—she knew they'd bitten her, just not how bad it really was. Falling on the ground in the cave had been a terrible mistake —an accident, sure, but still a mistake. *They're not normal spider bites, that's for sure,* she thought, finally looking down at herself to assess the damage.

Her legs looked like swollen, itchy masses attached to her body. The irritation called to her, begging her to dig her fingernails into her flesh, drag them across over and over, to relieve the feeling plaguing her. Unable to hold out any longer, Asia gave in to the urge.

The moment her nails pressed down into one of the sores, it burst open like a pimple. Yellow puss oozed out beneath her finger, mixed with something black. Asia grimaced at the disgusting sight, but she reached for her leg again. The relief was amazing—she had to scratch again, had to get rid of these sores making her leg look so nasty, she would *scrape* at herself until this feeling was gone.

She kept going faster, harder, deeper—not realizing she was ripping her skin clean off. Not realizing she was giving the spiders a way inside.

Asia closed her eyes to the pain, to the blood and the fluid. A scream came from the other side of the bathroom door, followed by another and another. Asia stopped—she finally opened her eyes to see what she was doing to herself.

She choked back a sob, watching the spiders climb out from beneath her skin, from *within* the sores that had been so itchy—begging her to release them. They crawled across her open flesh, looking for cover from the bathroom light, some looking for a way back inside *her*. A trail of them was traveling on the underside of her leg, staying close to her body to get to the gap beneath the bathroom door.

Asia screamed at the top of her lungs, kicking and flailing, swiping her hands across herself, trying to fling every one of the little creatures off her. Her toes stubbed against the cabinet, her freshly skinned shin hitting the toilet. She emitted a piercing howl, seeing nothing but the spiders on her body.

With one last burst of panic, Asia backed against the bathroom door, but she slipped in a pool of her own blood. Her arms flung out as she tried to catch herself, but she was too off-kilter. The back of her right hand slapped the light switch, sending her straight into darkness.

She fell hard, landing halfway in the bathtub as her head smacked the wall. A crack echoed within her skull —Asia wasn't sure if it was her head breaking or the RV —either way, it hurt like hell. The tub spout dug into what was left of her thigh, the shower curtain ripped off its flimsy rail, and a feeling of dizziness overcame her.

Asia felt the spiders immediately—there was no hesitation. They came out from within, looking for their meal now that they had the cover of darkness once again. The last thing she thought before she lost consciousness was, *I did this. I brought them here.*

IVEY and her family listened to Asia flailing in the bathroom, hearing one thud after another. They didn't understand what was happening until they spotted the first few spiders that crawled from beneath the door. Then, they watched in horror as what started off as a couple—turned into *many*.

"Hart—" Ivey said, unable to look away from the

spiders slinking through the shadows, wanting to hunt but wanting more to stay away from the light.

"We need more light," he said.

"Everything is on already."

Hart turned to his kids. "Grab anything you can think of. Xander, grab your flashlight and turn on your night-light. Kala, do the same."

"I don't have a night-light," Kala said.

"Use the light on your phone then! Anything, Kala, come on."

"Hart—will they be okay in there?" Ivey asked.

"They'll be fine. The spiders are coming from the bathroom—they were probably on Asia. She didn't go in the bunkhouse, so it's fine."

Ivey nodded toward her kids, who were both staring at the opening beneath the bathroom door with wide, terrified eyes. They'd have to walk past it to get to their room—the hallway was narrow, and no one knew if the spiders could or *would* try to jump on them.

"I'll shine a light over it," Ivey said, seeing their faces, knowing exactly what was going through her kids' minds. She grabbed the big flashlight that was normally kept near the front door and shined it directly at the darkest spot she could find.

The spiders fled faster than they came, scrambling back beneath the bathroom door into the protection of darkness. The few stragglers that remained shriveled in on themselves into a small, black dot that was barely perceptible. "Kill them with something, Hart," Ivey said, trying not to panic as the kids slipped past her into the bunkhouse.

"I'll go get the—" Hart started.

"No. No, you have to stay in here."

"It's just underneath—"

"Weren't you listening?" Ivey spun on him, almost moving the light from where it needed to be. "Those *things* are out there. They'll either get you or you'll bring them inside without knowing it. Either way, you have to stay here with us."

"Fine. I'll spray them with something else." He moved to look under the sink where she kept a few bottles full of cleaning supplies. He rummaged through them, then held one up toward her. "This has bleach in it—that should kill anything, right?"

It should, Ivey thought, *but will it?* "It's worth a try," she said. She turned back to look through the bunkhouse doorway—both her children were still searching for any lights they could find. The bathroom was quiet—too quiet. Ivey had a bad feeling about Asia. "Asia? Honey, are you okay?"

Asia didn't answer.

Xander found his lights first, rushing back out to the couch like he'd catch fire if he stayed too long.

Kala found hers a few seconds later, joining the rest of the family in the trailer's main living area.

With a shaking hand, Ivey reached for the bathroom door handle. "Asia?" she called again. When Asia still didn't answer, she knew she had to look, even if it was the last thing on earth she wanted to do. She twisted the handle—the door cracked open a sliver.

"Mom, be careful," Xander said. He, his dad, and his sister were all watching her with bated breath.

Ivey pulled the door open enough for her eye to see through. She gasped, stared—*couldn't stop* staring. The light from her flashlight was enough to send the spiders into hiding—but not totally. Asia's head and body were sideways in the tub, her legs twisted, hanging out. She was still naked—looked like she'd been nearly skinned alive.

And Ivey didn't miss the spiders crawling *inside* her —*eating* her. Webs were forming all over Asia's body, and from the glazed stare in her open eyes—Ivey knew she was dead.

She slammed the bathroom door shut, her whole body shuddering. A tingling sensation ran through her entire being, making her feel like the spiders were now on her, *in* her—they'd gotten inside her somehow and now she'd wind up the same way as Asia.

Ivey stood motionless, eyes clamped shut, hands clenched in a death grip around the flashlight.

"Hey, what is it?" Hart asked.

Ivey shook her head.

"Where is she?" Kala asked.

"She's—" Ivey choked. "She's—asleep."

Hart approached the wall beside Ivey, where the spiders were wrapped in on themselves. "Take this, you fuckers," he said, spraying the cleaner over and over until a puddle of it held all the black specs he could find.

"What do we do now?" Xander said.

"We get the hell out of here!" Kala cried, looking at him like he was crazy for not knowing.

"We can't," Hart said. "We don't know what's out there in the dark. We have to hunker down until morning."

"You want us to *sleep* here? With those things in the

bathroom?" Kala shrieked. Her face drained of all color as she looked between her parents. "We can't just leave Asia in there—"

"Stop!" Ivey cried. "Dad's right, Kala. We'll be okay as long as we have the lights on."

"You can't be serious!"

Ivey set the flashlight on the ground facing the gap beneath the bathroom door, then she moved to the couch to hold her children. "We'll be okay," she said again, holding them close to her, hoping with everything she had that she wasn't wrong.

After a quick peek into the bathroom, Hart took all the flashlights and any other light he could find and aimed them directly toward the bathroom door so there wasn't even a hint of a shadow for the spiders to reach.

NO ONE SLEPT A WINK. Morning came. The hours ticked by in the winter darkness, all of their bladders feeling like they'd explode, but all of them knew better than to step outside until it was full daylight.

When the time finally came, Hart was the first through the door, making sure the way was safe. Ivey led her children out the front door, leaving all their worldly possessions behind.

"Are we just going to leave her in the bathroom?" Kala asked.

"Yes," Ivey said.

"But—"

"Please, Kala."

Kala stopped asking questions.

The family piled into their old Dodge Ram and left their property as fast as the engine would take them, hitting the mailbox on their way out of the driveway, nearly knocking it to the ground.

PART III

7

L oreen pulled her mail truck off the side of the road, found the next stack of mail, shoved it in the box, then maneuvered her truck back onto the pavement, all without stopping. A car honked behind her, the driver flipping her the bird as he passed. "Nice fucking blinker!" he shouted through the window.

She only smiled. Angry drivers didn't bother her anymore. In fact, it pleased her every time she caused someone out there to have a little bit of road rage. *That's right, asshole,* she thought. *I have to get this done on a time limit and no one cares what you think! Enjoy your Saturday!*

Only, her boss *would* care. But that was okay because most people were too lazy to bother reporting her. They went on with their day as usual, and by the time they complained about her to a friend or remembered to report her, they couldn't even remember which road they were on or what day of the week it had been. At that point, they believed it didn't matter one way or another whether they left a complaint. Maybe it did, maybe it didn't, but Loreen knew one thing—she still had a job after all these years of doing the same thing.

She veered off the highway onto an old gravel road, grimacing as she finally came to the next stop on her route. *The fucking Hamiltons*, she thought, forcing herself to pull into the driveway and shut the truck off.

Just look at that mailbox! And people say I'm a bad driver! her mind cried when she saw the mailbox leaning forward, on the verge of collapse. The whole side of it was dented in like it had been hit by a car. With a groan, Loreen climbed out of the cab and walked past the leaning box to the edge of the property, where a small plastic storage shed was being used for packages.

The thing is supposed to be for garbage cans, not deliveries! she thought, raising the lid up. She held the top of it, while the bottom was supported by a narrow bar. Then Loreen dropped the box from chest level, smiling when she heard something break inside. *Oops*, she thought, oozing sarcasm, before slamming the lid of the container closed. It popped off the hinges, sitting sideways on top of the body of the container.

Loreen's smile widened to a grin. *Hope it doesn't rain*, she thought, seeing the dark-gray clouds in the sky overhead. *Maybe that will teach them to keep their mouths shut and not issue complaints for no reason. They have some nerve to try getting mail here at all! We weren't even supposed to be delivering to this property—God only knows why they're making me now with them living here in this forest—in a trailer—putting those kids through that! I've been doing this for twenty years and those trashy—*

"Ow!" she cried, cutting off the thought.

She looked down at the back of her hand to see a small black spider crawling across her. *The thing just bit me!* she thought, flinging her hand, shaking it wildly to get the spider off. When she saw it was gone, she climbed back in her mail truck, spitting rocks behind her as she backed out of the driveway.

Loreen continued on to the rest of her route, complaining similarly at each stop she came to. Someone was always leaving a complaint for her, bitching about one thing or another—and these were residents, not heated drivers. Their complaints were a whole different beast to deal with and she was getting fed up with having her boss on her ass every day.

It's not my job to drive up every goddamn dirt road to deliver packages! If the mailbox is at the end of the road, it's not my fault! And why are they always expecting me to get out in the rain and snow? It's not fair, not right that they don't appreciate me more, she thought.

Each stop she made brought on a fresh bout of anger because Loreen remembered each and every one who complained about her and *exactly* what the complaint was. The Walkers complained she kept delivering to the wrong address. Today, she chucked their box over their fence, watching it land in the bushes. *Oops,* she thought again, making a mental note to mention a locked gate if her boss brought this one up. *Let them chew on it,* Loreen thought, her mind laced with venom.

The Jones liked to bitch about how she *mishandled*

their deliveries, how they'd gotten so many *damaged* ones lately—like she was the only one putting her hands on their boxes. With a huff, she threw theirs out the window at the Cook house. *Gee, was that the wrong address? Oops, too late now!* she thought, glad once more that these people also had a gate she could use as an excuse. Matter of fact—didn't they have a dog too?

Later, she looked at her hand resting on the steering wheel, noticing a red lump forming where the spider had bitten her earlier. Anger flared up again at the memory. *If I didn't have to get out and open that goddamn container, this would've never happened.* Loreen absently held the steering wheel with her injured hand while she used the other to scratch at the bite. She winced at the pain, drawing back. *I should insist that it's a hazard to keep going there. I should refuse to go back—make them pay me hazard pay!*

GOING on and on to herself the rest of her route, Loreen had plenty she was upset about, plenty she wanted to say but no one to say it to. There was only one other driver at their small-town post office, and he got the in-town residents. Loreen was forced out to the boon-docks, where all the people on the outskirts hated her guts. *If only Tegan would trade with me,* she thought on her way back to turn her truck in for the night.

Tegan has all the best people. They're so kind—so appre-

ciative. Maybe I need to be the one to file a complaint about favoritism within this town's branch.

As she parked, she noticed the red bite mark on the back of her hand again. *It looks worse,* she thought, bringing her other hand over to poke at it, grimacing as yellow puss oozed out of it like a pimple. Loreen tried to flex her hand, but the pain was too much to bear. *Great, just what I need!* she thought, climbing out of the mail truck for the last time that day.

She made her way inside the building to clock out and turn in her keys, keeping her hurt hand stiff next to her side the whole time. Tegan's keys were already there—he always seemed to be off before her. *I bet he doesn't have to suffer any damn bug bites.* Color flooded her face as a bitter resentment reared its ugly head. Loreen left the building without a word to anyone.

8

L oreen woke in the night from the pain in her right hand. It felt like something inside was pulsing, clawing, eating away at her very tendons. She wiped the cold sweat from her brow, reaching to flip on the lamp beside the bed.

For a moment, she forgot to use her good hand. She reached with her right—crying out from the pain of trying to manipulate her index finger. *Holy hell, what kind of spider was it?* She wondered, realizing she wasn't reacting well to whatever kind of venom it'd injected in her hand.

She finally managed to get the bedside lamp on and gasped when she got a good look at her hand. All five of her fingers looked like fat red sausages, shiny from being so swollen. The bite itself now seemed to take up the entire back of her hand, forming a massive red pustule.

Loreen's hand shook as she analyzed herself. Fury bubbled up inside her again, remembering the

Hamilton family that made her put their packages in that fucking plastic shed. *They should be the ones with this, not me! This is their fault! All their fault! Someone needs to complain to the county, to CPS! Someone needs to report them and get them out of that RV and off of that land! If they could've just kept their mouths shut and let me do my job!*

In her anger, she began to tighten her right hand into a fist without realizing it. Pain shot up her arm, past her elbow, clear to her shoulder. The movement stretched her skin, causing the pustule to burst open. Thick yellow fluid oozed out of her, making her gag at the sight and the smell of it.

Loreen looked away, unable to bear the sight anymore. Then she felt something else on the back of her hand—something other than the puss. It felt almost like—

Loreen turned back, eyes growing wide at the sight. Spiders. There were spiders crawling out from the inside of her hand, moving down her fingers and up her arm.

She screamed a bloodcurdling cry. "Get off, get off, get off!" She forgot all about the pain, consumed by the thought of getting the spiders off of her, *out* of her. Loreen flung her right hand around wildly, clawing at herself with her left.

Puss, blood, and spiders sprayed over her body, the bed, and the room. She stood, rushing for the light switch across the room. As she did, her mind spun with dizziness. She looked down to see even more spiders crawling out from inside her hand, covered in her blood and bodily fluids. The farther away from the lamp, the dimmer the light, and the more active the tiny spiders became.

She gagged but couldn't hold back any longer. Vomit flew from her mouth onto her open wound, covering the spiders and herself in stomach waste. She gagged again at the sight, over and over until tears sprang from the corners of her eyes.

Loreen wanted to scream again but couldn't. She was too weak, her throat too raw. The pain in her hand was excruciating, like she'd rather have it sawed off than have to go through this anymore.

Finally, she reached the switch, flipped it, and lit up the room. She paused, hating to look, but mesmerized by the way the spiders were reacting to the light. They weren't coming out of her anymore—instead, they were trying to crawl back inside.

There was a moment when she was frozen—physically incapable of movement. She stared at the spiders who had been melted by her stomach acid, at the others who were crawling around their melted comrades, seeking shelter back inside her body. *Are they hissing?* she wondered. Then, *this isn't real. This isn't happening. I have a fever. That's all.*

The pain came back, hitting Loreen at full force. It finally dawned on her what was happening—that these creatures were inside of her body. She had to stop them. She had to get them out!

Loreen flung the door open, running for the kitchen as fast as her body would carry her. She pulled a knife from the drawer and started to dig.

THE PARAMEDICS CAME, alerted by a neighbor who was awoken by the sound of Loreen's screams. They busted down the door to get inside, finding Loreen on the kitchen floor in a pool of her own blood. She had a knife in her left hand—gouging into her right hand like she was searching for buried treasure.

Her hand was mutilated into a mass of bloody meat —cut ten ways to Sunday, beyond all recognition of what a hand should be. The paramedics moved to help her, to get the knife from her, but she brandished it like a sword, warning them off. "I have to get them out!" she screamed. "I can't leave them inside me!"

"You got them," one of the paramedics said. "Look." He pointed to her hand, trying to make her see what she was doing to herself, while the other alerted the police that they may need some help with the weapon.

Loreen looked back down at her hand, not seeing what they saw. What she saw—was the possibility of *more* of them coming out of her. "I think there's more," she said, wary, wanting to believe him but not quite there.

"You definitely got them. I promise."

"Are you sure? How do you know?"

This lady has lost so much blood—how is she even conscious? the paramedic thought before saying, "It's my job." He pointed to his uniform.

Loreen came out of her daze a little. She realized

that they were there to help her, to get the spiders out of her—gone forever. "How did you know to come?" she asked. She tried to stand but was too weak.

"Hey, let us help you, okay? We just need you to put the knife down."

Loreen looked at the knife, back down at her hand, then up at the two paramedics waiting to help her. She wanted to let them. She wanted to hand it off to them— let them kill the little fuckers, get them all out of her, every single one. She was so tired, could hardly keep her eyes open. "Promise you'll get them all," she said, dropping the knife.

She passed out where she sat, and they moved to help her.

9

Loreen woke with a start. She thought she was back in her kitchen with the knife, still digging them out. *I have to get them out!* she thought, panic rising again. The sound of the heart rate monitor beside her bed pulled her into reality. She looked around the room, realizing she wasn't at home —she was in a hospital.

She looked down at her hand, then screamed.

A nurse ran into the room. "It's okay, Loreen. You're safe," he said, coming over to press some buttons on the monitor. He looked down at her with sympathy, but Loreen didn't see any of that. All she saw—was that her hand was gone.

"Where is it?" she cried. "Where the fuck is my hand!"

"Just calm down for a minute, please, Loreen. I'll explain everything."

"You better goddamn well explain! I'm going to sue!

I'm going to have your fucking head on a platter! I'm going to—"

The nurse injected a sedative into her IV bag. It only took a few moments for it to drip down into Loreen's vein and send her spiraling back to sleep.

She woke with a start again. But this time she remembered. Loreen looked down at her arm—her *stump*, where her hand should be. Tears welled in her eyes. Then the anger came—red, hot, and out of control. *This is all their fault*, she said, *that fucking family in their RV, and their complaints against me. If they would've just kept their mouths closed!*

Nausea rose in Loreen's throat. She swallowed it back down, wiped the tears from her eyes, and forced herself to take a deep breath. Payback could wait. There was only one thing that mattered right now—one simple thing, more than anything else in the world. Did they get *all* the spiders out of her?

She imagined two of the tiny little arachnids left over, burrowed deep within her arm. She imagined them mating and laying a sac filled with eggs—more little spider babies to eat her alive from the inside out.

Loreen was growing sweaty again. She felt itchy—under her hair, along her back, *in her arm*. She used her good hand to rub at her skin and hair while she twisted in her bed in a desperate attempt to erase the feeling. It wasn't working. She dug her nails into her skin, scratching harder, then even harder, savoring the burn because it meant *they* weren't there.

She eyed the bandage on her arm. *Just one little peek*, she thought before she grabbed hold of the edge of it and began ripping it away from her body.

THE NURSE CHECKED HIS WATCH, brows furrowed. It had been a few hours since he dosed Loreen with the sedative. *She should be awake by now. Why is it so quiet in there?* he thought. He admonished himself for getting caught up in his rounds and not checking back on her sooner, then, with a sinking feeling in his gut, he headed toward her room.

He knocked twice, calling, "Loreen, are you awake?" There was a glow of light from inside—he saw that much. It wasn't unusual for patients to sleep with the light on, but it was turned off when he last left.

No answer came, so the nurse entered the room.

Loreen was awake alright, sitting beneath the glow of the fluorescent lights. She was sitting up in bed, ripping at her open wound with her left hand and with her teeth. Bits of flesh and blood were splattered across her chest and face, blood dripping down her residual arm.

He held a hand up to his mouth, frozen by the sight of the woman ripping herself apart. She looked up at him, baring her teeth, blood running down her face and chin. "You didn't get them all!" she cried. "I *knew*

you didn't! They don't like the light! They dig themselves deeper down—you have to dig for them!"

The nurse hit his panic button, then he rushed to
stop her.

Loreen fought tooth and nail, but she was no match
for the man who was nearly twice her size. Within a
few moments, other nurses responded to the struggle,
along with hospital security. They were able to get
Loreen sedated once more, restraining her this time
with straps across her body.

PART IV

10

A cross the hospital, Rafe sat in the emergency room waiting area, nursing a leg he hoped wasn't broken. He checked his watch, wondering how many more hours it would be before someone could come give it a look. *I should just go home. It's probably just sprained,* he thought, trying to convince himself that it wasn't worth his time to be waiting around like this doing nothing.

An alarm went off on the hospital PA system. Security guards rushed to the stairwell and a moment later, Rafe saw police rushing through the hospital doors. *Holy shit, what's going on?* he wondered, seeing the panic on their faces.

Nurses and other staff were in a flurry, answering phones, making calls, some following after police in security in the elevators. Then, all was quiet again, back to normal.

Rafe looked around the waiting room, noting that there were a few others waiting who were also curious, but the majority looked like they couldn't care less what was going on. There were some who hadn't even noticed the commotion at all.

A nurse came from behind a door, calling his name. There was a moment when Rafe didn't want to stand. He wanted to stay here and wait to see who the police brought back out with them. *This has got to be good!* he thought, then he remembered the pain in his leg and how long he'd been waiting.

"Rafe Roberts," the nurse called again.

Ah hell, Rafe thought. *It'll probably take them another hour to get back down here anyway.* "I'm here," he called to the nurse. He grabbed his crutches and stood with a groan, trying not to put any weight on his hurt leg.

The nurse led him to a bed where she took his vitals and assessed the damage. When she determined he wasn't about to die, she asked him to wait for the doctor, then left him alone. Minutes ticked by as Rafe again questioned the wisdom of spending his entire Saturday evening at the hospital. *I could be at the house doing something. The emergency room is for people dying, not this*—he thought, looking down at his busted leg.

On the other side of the curtain, a couple of nurses were having a heated conversation. "What the hell were they thinking, not restraining her in the first place?" one said.

"You know it's at the doctor's discretion. He didn't think it would be necessary," the second said.

"She was half-crazy when the paramedics found her! Her hand was practically sawn off—what did they think she was going to do when she woke up?"

Rafe's eyebrows rose. *I bet that's what all the fuss was*

about—whatever patient they're talking about. He held perfectly still, hoping the doctor wouldn't come in the middle of their conversation.

"Well, she about bled out when Ray found her, from what I understand," the second nurse said.

"Why on earth did they leave her alone like that?"

"Ray said she was sedated. How was he supposed to know she was off her rocker?"

There was a moment of silence, then the first nurse's voice came again from farther away. "Whatever drugs she was on must've been strong as hell," the first nurse said. "To believe that *spiders* were in her arm, eating her from the inside out—lord almighty."

They were too far now for Rafe to hear any more of the conversation. He sat reeling at what he'd just heard. *Her hand was practically sawn off—spiders eating her from the inside out—Jesus Christ, the shit these people have to deal with*, he thought with newfound respect. *I might've gone screaming in the other direction if I came across a lady like that.*

A few minutes later, the doctor came by to give Rafe's leg a look over. "Wow, what happened here?" she asked when she saw the open gash on his outer thigh. It had been hours, but blood was still slightly leaking from the wound when he moved it for her to get a better view. She prodded the spot he thought might be broken, making Rafe wince and pull back.

"I fell off the ladder," he said.

"You're lucky it's not worse," she said, twisting it.

Rafe flinched again. "It sure hurts like hell. You think it's broken?"

"No, not broken, but the bone is most likely bruised.

You'll need some stitches." She looked up from the wound to meet his eyes. "I don't think you need an X-ray, but would you feel better having one?"

"I'll take your word for it," Rafe said, relieved it wasn't as bad as he'd thought.

She nodded. "You'll need to take it easy for a few weeks. What were you doing up on a ladder?"

"I'm fixing up a house my uncle left me. It's out in the middle of nowhere, hard to get help to come all the way out for every little thing and I'm hoping to turn a profit if I can."

"Well, I advise you to stay off that leg as much as possible. It's going to need time to heal."

"I'll do the best I can," Rafe said.

WHEN RAFE GOT HOME from the hospital, his uncle's little dog—*his* little dog now, was waiting for him. The black mini pinscher barked at his feet, yipping and wagging her tail excitely the minute he stepped through the front door. "Sorry, Boo girl, I know I was gone a while." He laughed when she licked at his jeans and stood on her back paws, looking up at him with her big brown eyes.

"You're lucky you're such a small thing," he said, balancing the crutches so he could lean down and pick her up with a swoop. The dog licked the stubble on his cheek, wagging her tail so hard it hurt when she whipped it against him.

Rafe kissed the top of her head, ruffled her ears and fur, then continued into the kitchen to grab a beer. It was a challenge trying to balance with one crutch, holding the dog, and not putting any weight on his hurt leg. Each step he took felt like nails driven into his thigh, but he had no one there to help. He had to do what he had to do.

"It's not broken, girl," he said to Boo.

She licked his cheek again like she understood.

Rafe made his way to the couch, plopping down with the dog and the drink. *What the hell am I going to do now?* He slid his hand over Boo's back, twisting her short black hair between his fingers, rubbing her velvet ears as he thought about his choices.

There's so much to do still... I've barely gotten started, he thought, looking around, seeing all the things that needed to be repaired. *Damn, Uncle, what were you thinking letting this place go to hell?* He began naming off all the things that stood out on the first floor alone. "Fix the windows, new paint, new carpet, fix the leak in the kitchen, take care of the rot by the front door, replace the cracked bathroom door..." The list went on and on.

Night was on the other side of the old, cracked living room window. Rafe eyed the lamp on the other side of the room, wanting anything in the world but to have to get up off the couch in order to turn it on. "You wouldn't want to go flip the switch, would you, girl?" he asked Boo with a smile.

She panted up at him, tilting her head like she was trying to figure out what he wanted.

With a sigh, he said, "It's okay. I'll get it." He worked his way slowly back up and over to the lamp, gritting his teeth against the pain. The lamp wasn't the brightest thing in the house, but with the new LED bulb he put in it, it was good enough to light the area for the time being.

When it flicked on, Rafe noticed a few small black spiders on the floor near its base, scurrying away from the light. *Better call the pest guy tomorrow. I hope he'll come out on a Sunday*, he thought, squishing one under his crutch. The others disappeared from the light as fast as he'd seen them, off into the bowels of the house. "Don't worry, friends. I'll take care of you tomorrow," Rafe said.

He checked the time on his watch. "Come on, Boo, better get some dinner and make ourselves comfortable. We're going to be staying downstairs for a while."

The little dog hopped down off the couch, heading to the kitchen at the sound of *dinner*. She stopped in the doorway, looking back at Rafe as if to ask, *are you coming or what?*

"I'm coming, I'm coming," he said, heading after her.

11

The pest guy turned off the gravel road, heading down the long dirt driveway, over-grown with weeds. *Jeez, someone needs to spray*, he thought, trying to determine where the actual driveway was—he thought he might be halfway on the yard because it was so badly overgrown. A few seconds later, an old two-story house came into view. He parked near the front porch, grabbing his clipboard and climbing out.

A man on crutches came out to meet him, a little black dog by his side. "Hello, I'm Warren Bailey, the pest guy. Are you Rafe?"

"That's me. Glad you're here so fast. Thanks for squeezing me in on a Sunday."

"My pleasure. You're the last stop of the day, so no sweat off my back." He held up his clipboard. "I'm just going to take a few notes about things that stand out, then I'll give you an estimate and you can decide if you want to move forward with a treatment service."

Rafe nodded. "Do your thing. I'll just be on the porch if you need me."

Warren looked down at the little dog by Rafe's side. "Is he nice?"

Rafe looked down at her too. "Oh yeah, she's a sweetheart. Might bark a little is all."

Warren didn't normally like dealing with dogs—especially ones that weren't fenced or on a leash, but this dog was small—had to be only fifteen pounds, maybe less. She seemed harmless enough. He nodded, deciding not to make a fuss about it.

He checked his notes on his clipboard from when Rafe's call came through to the office. "The problem areas are the front porch and under the eaves. Is that correct?"

"Yes. I saw some spiders inside, too."

"Alrighty. I think I'll take a look in the crawlspace first."

Rafe showed him the access door before moving back to the porch to wait with his dog.

BENEATH THE HOUSE WAS A MESS. *Gonna be a big job here*, Warren thought, glad he'd agreed to take this last stop for the day. This wouldn't be a one-treatment house, no sir. He'd have to come back multiple times to make an impact on this situation.

Rafe had mentioned spiders, but Warren was seeing much more than that. There were molehills, feces, and a couple of different nests—signs of all kinds of different rodents and pests living under there. There were so many cobwebs Warren could hardly crawl forward without having to clear them out of the way.

At least it's dry, Warren thought. Dry was always a good sign. He scanned the area for points of access, stopping every now and then to jot a note or two on his board. After a few minutes, he climbed back out from under the house and took a look around the outside perimeter, adding more notes as he went.

"I have some good news and bad," he reported to Rafe.

"Give it to me."

"Lots of activity down there, but I can definitely pinpoint how they're getting under there and we can stop it."

"That's what I like to hear." Rafe nodded.

"Alright, good. I'll move inside now, if that's alright."

"Absolutely." Rafe ushered him inside through the front door. He pointed out the spots he'd noticed with his own untrained eye, then let Warren continue having a look on his own.

Ten minutes later, Warren came back out to report what he'd found. "I just had a quick peek—didn't go up to the attic or anything. I think I saw enough as it is to have a good idea of what we're dealing with."

"Did you see a lot?"

"Some. But it was more the signs of their presence that I'm worried about. I'll work up a bid and email it over in the morning."

"I'll be honest, Warren. This is a renovation project. I'm trying to get this all taken care of as soon as possible so I can get it off my hands. Whatever you can do for me to get this taken care of quickly—I want it."

Warren nodded. "Alright. In that case, I'll work up the bid anyway, but I'll get you on the schedule in the meantime."

"How soon do you think you can make it back out?"

"Well, we've been having a lot of calls come in lately..." He scratched his head, thinking about how full the schedule was.

"I'd be willing to pay extra to get it done sooner."

Warren smiled. "I normally don't do this, but I like you. I may be able to squeeze you in tomorrow."

Rafe nodded. "That sounds like a good deal to me."

They shook hands before Rafe went back inside with his little dog by his side and Warren got back in his truck, heading home for the day.

AFTER A LONG DAY, Warren was glad to pull into his own driveway with dinner in hand. The Teriyaki smelled so good it was making his mouth water. It was hot and ready, waiting for him to devour it the second he could get inside.

Business was damned good today. I'll have to get my assistant to get Rafe scheduled before I forget, Warren thought with a smile, turning off the truck and stepping out. He loved this time of year—the spiders creeping their way inside homes to hide for the cold months. They made business boom enough to get him through the slower parts of the year. While everyone else had Sunday off, he took advantage of the busiest day of the week for making money.

Warren walked around the hood of his truck to cross his driveway when a shrill voice called his name. "Warren! You're home late today!"

He turned to see his neighbor, Jewell, watching him from her front porch. With a silent groan, Warren waved. "Busy day today, Jewell. Have a nice evening!" He kept moving toward the front door, thinking, *Mind your own business, you nosy bitch.*

"Wait just a minute!" she cried, slowly standing and making her way to the hedges that bordered their properties.

Warren's heart spasmed for a moment. *Did I just say that out loud?* he thought. Then he looked down to his warm, delicious food, waiting for him. His stomach rumbled, begging him to ignore Jewell, to get inside before she gave him a headache he didn't need.

His sense of propriety won. As much as he hated to stand here and listen to her, he knew it was the right thing to do—at least for a minute. He was her neighbor after all, and she was just a lonely woman who had nothing else to do but complain. He would indulge her for sixty seconds.

Jewell made it to the hedges, huffing. "I've been seeing a lot of bugs lately," she started.

Warren nodded. "Most people have. It's the time of year—they all go scurrying for places to hide as the weather cools down."

"Well, they're not going to hide in my house, that's for sure."

He smiled. "Most people feel the same, I think."

"When are you going to have a chance to spray?"

"Just call the office and we'll set up an appointment any time there's an opening. It's going to be pretty busy this week—lots of calls coming in lately, so you might want to call as soon as possible."

Jewel's eyebrows shot up. "I don't have time to do that."

Warren was stunned for a moment, not quite sure what to say. "If you want an appointment, you'll need to call to schedule. That's how it works." His bag of food felt heavy in his hands, and his stomach rumbled again. Warren looked down at it longingly. He started to raise it up to show her he needed to go eat his dinner, he didn't have any more time for her trying to take advantage of him, but she cut him off.

"We're neighbors," Jewell said matter-of-factly. "Why should I have to make an appointment?"

"I'm not going to spray your home for free."

She looked like he'd slapped her. "We're neighbors," she said again.

Warren sighed. This conversation was old already. "I'm going to go eat my dinner, Jewell," he said. "It's been nice talking to you." He started to walk away, back toward his front door. *This was not worth letting my food go cold. Nothing I do is going to please her anyway!*

"I can't believe this!" Jewell cried. "I can't believe you'd treat your neighbor in such a way. I'm going to call and complain! I'm going to tell everyone I know how terrible your customer service is, Warren Bailey!"

He stuck his key in his front door, ignoring every angry word she spewed.

12

Jewell couldn't believe her ears. She was so in shock from the way Warren had treated her she stood there staring after him with her jaw dropped. *That man has gotten too big for his britches!* She clenched her fists by her side. *We'll see how fast he makes an attitude adjustment once I get through with him!*

She turned to go back inside, mortified to be denied in such a public way. She didn't even want to look over her shoulder and see the other neighbors who might've witnessed Warren put her down like that. *That he wouldn't even offer to set traps for me! And knowing I have those damned pests that keep coming back! Or a simple spray around the house? How hard could that really be?* she thought, shaking her head.

Inside the house, her cat meowed at her from his perch by the front window. "Shadow, you should've seen it. He was awful to me," Jewell said, moving to scratch her nails along his back. He purred beneath her fingers as she went on. "What use is having a neighbor anyway? There used to be a time when neighbors did things for each other. They didn't make them *call and schedule appointments!*" Her face crumpled in disgust.

"To make your neighbor *pay*, Shadow! And have to *wait* like a common customer. We've been neighbors for *years!* We're practically family! I mean, I see him more than my own kids!"

Shadow stopped purring and stood. He whipped his tail against her cheek, then walked off.

"Oh, fine. I'm done with it anyway," Jewell said. She made herself comfortable on the couch, found her favorite show on TV, and lost herself in another world for a short while.

JEWELL WENT through her normal evening routine—brushing her teeth and hair, taking her pills, putting on facial moisturizer, changing into her nightgown, and grabbing a novel before climbing into bed. She wiggled down beneath the plush, down comforter, resting her head against three pillows, then opened her book and began to read.

Shadow slinked through the darkened room, eventually jumping up to lie on the bed beside her. Jewell stroked his back and tail with her long nails again, just the way he liked, drawing out the low purring from his chest and throat. They stayed like that together until Jewell was too tired to see straight. She set her book and glasses on the night table beside the bed and turned off her lamp to go to sleep.

A noise came from above. The ceiling creaked. Jewell's eyes flew open, staring into the black room. A scuttling noise—*something is up there*, she thought.

Shadow made a curious chirping noise. Jewell could see his silhouette on the bed, looking up toward the ceiling. *So I'm not going crazy. There really is something up there*, she thought. She turned to slam an open palm against the wall behind her bed.

The sound from above stopped. She released a sigh of relief, glad she wouldn't have to hear—there it was again. It was closer now—sounded like—Jewell squinted into the dark room, trying to focus, trying to pinpoint what on earth was making that terrible noise.

She waited for the sound to come again. There! *There's more than one!* she thought, listening carefully to what sounded like several tiny feet above. *Just wait until Warren hears about this! This is all his damned fault! If he would just help me—now I'm not going to be able to sleep!*

"Shadow, would you do your damned job, cat? Someone needs to around here."

He lay there, staring at the ceiling.

With a sigh, Jewell pulled one of the pillows from beneath her head and covered her face and ears with it, trying to drown out the noise. "Go away!" she cried, slapping her palm against the wall again.

Shadow jumped off the bed and left the room, leaving Jewell alone. She closed her eyes, trying to focus on listening to the sound of her own breathing. Eventually she was able to pass out.

SHE WOKE WITH A START, sitting up in a panic. *Why was there a pillow on my face?* she thought. Then she heard scratching from in the wall behind her head and remembered. She spun, staring at the wall with a horrified look. Whatever had been in the ceiling was working its way down. She wanted to slap the wall again, remembering that it brought her a moment's peace—but was too afraid to touch it.

What if whatever's in there is able to break through? she wondered, scooting farther away until she was sitting at the foot of the bed. She stared into the night, listening to the occasional skittering up the walls. The sounds still came from the roof too—a scratching or a skittering every few seconds.

Jewell reached for the lamp, not wanting to be in the dark anymore. This infestation was worse than she'd imagined. *It's like they're multiplying,* she thought.

The light brought her some relief—made her feel less alone somehow. She looked around the room for her cat, but he hadn't come back in the room yet. "Shadow?" Jewell called toward the doorway. He was a good cat, always slept by her side, normally came when called too—but she admitted he was still a cat with a mind of his own. *Don't leave me alone now, boy,* she thought.

She listened. There had been no more sounds in the last few seconds. Slowly, carefully, Jewell moved back toward the wall. She hovered near it, waiting again for the sounds to come.

They've stopped, she thought. Then she wondered, *Why have they stopped?* Jewell eased closer to the wall, pressing her ear against it to listen. She closed her eyes, waiting again for the movement to come.

"They're gone," she said aloud. "Oh, thank God." She placed a hand to her chest, took a few heavy breaths, then made herself comfortable in bed once again.

She reached over, turned the lamp back off, and went back to sleep.

JEWELL DIDN'T KNOW how long it was before she woke to the sounds again. She stared red-eyed at the ceiling before sitting up to twist and look back at the wall. *This is bullshit!* she thought, growing furious—not with the bugs, but with Warren.

This was *his* fault. He could easily put a stop to it, but he wouldn't—he didn't want to. *He should be the one forced to listen to them all night, not me,* she thought, gripping the sheet tight in her fist. She ripped the covers off herself and reached to flick the light back on.

The scampering stopped. She waited, straining to listen.

Nothing.

No—there—

It stopped.

Whatever it is, it doesn't like the light, Jewell thought. Then—*How can it see the light from inside there?* She looked more closely at the wall, then up at the ceiling. She couldn't figure it out but was too tired to try anymore. It didn't matter. What mattered was that their movement slowed down—if not stopped altogether with the lights on.

Jewell got out of bed to flip on every light in the house. Only when the house was a glowing beacon in the night was she satisfied. Jewell went back to bed, putting a pillow over her eyes.

PART V

13

Ivey hadn't allowed anyone to touch a single light in the motel room all weekend. Every bulb had stayed on, including the one in the closet. There wasn't a square inch not illuminated by artificial light, but no one said a word in protest. Instead, they were worried about one of the lights burning out and allowing even a sliver of darkness.

She and Hart had both called into work while keeping the kids home from school. The image of Asia in their tub haunted her every waking hour, and the thought that her children could wind up that way was too much to take. She refused to send them anywhere without her until she knew for a fact it was safe.

"We need to stop and get backup lights," Hart said.

Ivey looked around the room. "Do you think they'll go out? We're not going to be here that long, are we?"

He shrugged. "I don't know. But better to be safe, isn't it? What if those fuckers are still in the RV and they get out and—"

"Dad!" Xander cried.

"Sorry, son. I didn't mean to use such foul language."

"No, it's not that. It's—do you really think they'll follow us?" His eyes roamed the room with a new lens.

"Why don't we get out of here?" Kala cried. "I don't understand! I can still feel them on me! We need to leave this place." She ran her hands over her arms, shuddering at the memory of what they'd narrowly escaped.

"All we have left in the world is in this town, Kala. We can't just abandon it," Hart said. He turned to Xander. "They're gone. They're all gone. But, in case there's a straggler—it's better to be safe."

"So, we're supposed to live the rest of our lives with the lights on?" Kala asked. "Never go back to school?"

"Only for now. Until we can get an exterminator out to the RV."

"What about Asia?" Kala insisted. She gave her parents a look that said, *I know she's not okay.*

"We'll call the police, along with an exterminator. Everything will be taken care of, then we'll go back." Hart looked at each of his family. "We should be glad the house isn't done yet. I know you don't want to hear this, but imagine if we had to deal with this inside a permanent home."

"How do we *know* they're not here? How are we so sure? You saw those things! Asia carried them on her—what if they hitched a ride on one of us too?" Kala cried, unable to drop it.

"Alright. I think we all could use some fresh air," Ivey said. "You're right, Kala, we need to get out of here for a while. Let's go to the store and grab some things. We can stop and grab a few groceries while we're at it."

"So, you're just going to ignore me? That's it?"

Ivey and Hart shared a look. Hart said, "We haven't seen a sign of them since we left the property. They're not here. We don't know anything for certain—but we have a pretty good idea. And like I said before, we need to get the pest guy out to the property." He looked at Ivey again then back to his daughter. "We need to get some fresh air. Running a few errands will do us good."

For once, Kala didn't have something smart to say in response. The family filed out of the motel room door, glad to have a plan and glad to be getting out.

NONE of them wanted to go back to the motel—what would be the point? Just to sit there with the lights glaring in their eyes, fearing a spider making its way inside through one of the shadows? They all knew they had to plug in the extra lights before any burned out, whether they wanted to or not. Like Hart had said—*it's better to be safe.*

The last stop for the afternoon was the grocery store. "Hart, Xander, if you two want to stay in the truck, Kala and I will only be a few minutes," Ivey said as they parked.

"Why do I have to go?" Kala asked.

"Because you know what to look for. Please, Kala, I need your help."

"We'll stay here. It'll be easier for you guys if we're out of the way," Hart said. He looked to Xander, who nodded his agreement.

"Okay. We're going to be quick. I want to get back to plug those lights in."

Ivey told Kala what to look for in the produce section while she headed to the opposite end of the store. They didn't need much—but she wanted to make sure they had enough food once night fell. Part of her was terrified to leave the motel at dark, knowing those spiders could be out there anywhere, creeping through the night, preying on those too ignorant to know better than to stay inside.

I'm glad the boys stayed in the truck. We'll be in and out in a flash, she thought.

Two minutes after the girls left, Hart held a hand to his stomach, cringing at the pain.

Xander watched him from the corner of his eye, understanding what was about to happen. "The bathroom is probably in the back," he said.

"I'll be fine. I—oh!" He doubled over in his seat, clutching at his stomach, groaning.

"Dad, maybe you should—"

Hart unfastened his seat belt. "I'm sorry, Xander. I'll try to be fast. Here are the keys." He threw the keys to Xander in the back seat before getting out and shuffling into the store in search of the bathroom.

He really needs to see a doctor one of these days, Xander thought, watching his dad leave.

IN THE PRODUCE SECTION, Kala grabbed a basket to put the fresh fruits and vegetables in. First on the list was lettuce, so she moved over to that area, waiting for the sprinklers to turn off so she could make her selection without getting wet. *I don't see why they always have to have salad. All we ever do is throw half of it away,* she thought.

The sprinklers turned off. Kala looked for the fresh cuts of Romaine that her mom liked to buy, moved a few from the top of the stack, grabbed fresher ones below, and added them to her basket. *There, Mom, you happy?* Water from the freshly watered vegetables dropped through an open hole in her basket, landing on her shoe with a soft splat.

Kala looked down, saw the water, and realized she had forgotten one of the plastic produce bags. She looked around the nearby area, spotting a roll of them near the apples. *Mom said to grab some of those too,* she thought, moving to tear a few bags from the roll.

She felt her phone buzz in her pocket—ignored it, thinking it was just her mom telling her to hurry up. *I still don't see why we have to stay in that motel,* she thought with disgust. Part of her wanted to throw a fit like a toddler until she got her way, another part wanted to run away so she wouldn't have to deal with this—let her parents handle it. But there was an even darker part—a stronger part—that thought her parents might be right about the lights. If she ran away, would she be able to stay in the light? She wasn't so sure—at least not all the time. And if there was one thing Kala believed, it was that the light was safe from those *things* —it was the one thing Asia had insisted upon.

Kala's phone vibrated again as she reached for the apples. She stopped, shifted the basket on her arm, and looked to see who it was.

Her mom, just like she'd expected.

> I'm grabbing one last thing. Meet me up front.

What did she grab? Two things? Kala thought, slipping her phone back into her pocket. Her outstretched hand moved a few apples on autopilot. She didn't have to look to know her mom never wanted her to take from the top of the stack.

Her fingertips brushed a stem. Her eyes drifted— finally meeting what she was touching. The breath was stolen from her lungs. In a split second, she found air and emitted a screech that could be heard clear inside the men's bathroom at the back of the store. "Get it off! Get it off!" she cried, whipping her hand back and forth so violently she could hear the bones in her wrist protest.

One of those *spiders* was here—it was inside the grocery store! Kala saw it crawl beneath the apples, hiding from the glowing fluorescent lights. She yelled again and again, backing from the apples but unable to tear her eyes from them.

They're here. They're here. How did they get here? Did we carry them in? Are they in the motel room? Are they still in my hair? she thought, her mind spinning out of control.

Kala looked at her hands to make sure—then she ran them through her hair, flipping it and whipping it, kneading her fingers down to her scalp. She felt something—shrieked again, a guttural cry for help. "Mooom!" Tears came, hot and thick, down her cheeks. She danced around the produce section like a maniac —batting her head, pulling her hair, jerking forward and back, and at all angles, panicked and desperate to get the *thing* off her.

"Someone help me! The spiders are here! They came from the cave—they're going to kill us! They don't like the light! You have to turn on more lights!"

Ivey came running from across the store, saw her daughter, and realized immediately what was happening. She ignored the other patrons staring wide eyed and the gaping employees who were unsure what to do. She moved to her daughter, putting a hand on her arm to calm her. "I'm here," she said.

Kala turned to her with wild hair and eyes, snot and tears covering her face. "One of them is on me, Mommy! Get it off!" she shrieked.

"Where? Where is it, Kala?"

"My hair!" she trembled, wanting to scratch at her head until it was raw, wanting to gouge her fingers down to the very bone just to erase any trace of the arachnid.

Ivey reached for her daughter's head, pushing her down so she could get a better view. She flipped through Kala's hair like an expert. "This is just like the time you had lice in kindergarten all those years ago. You remember that?"

"You're not helping!" Kala cried.

"Sorry. Look, honey, I don't see the spider. It's gone."

Kala wiped her eyes. "No. No, I felt it."

"You must've felt this," Ivey said, holding up a small piece of bread from lunch that'd wedged itself into the strands.

"No. No, I'm telling you. I saw one of them! There was one in my hair! I felt it!"

"I believe you. But Kala, it's not in your hair now. I promise."

Kala looked around, finally seeing all the staring eyes. She began to cry again, embarrassed and ashamed.

Ivey pulled her close. Then, she turned back toward the employees. "What do you have to say for yourselves? There are *bugs* in the produce! *Spiders!* You see how it affected my daughter!" She turned toward the other shoppers. "I'd be wary before buying produce here ever again. I'm not going to shop somewhere where they let *insects* crawl all over my food!"

"Spiders aren't insects—" someone called back.

"Don't be a smart-ass. Does that really matter?" someone else called.

A few employees moved toward the apples.

"Don't!" Kala cried. "They're in there!"

They looked to her and then back toward the apples, fear at what they'd find etched on their faces.

"Come on. We're leaving," Ivey whispered in Kala's ear.

"We can't just leave them—"

"We can. And we're going to," Ivey hissed.

She grabbed the basket from Kala's arm, set it on the ground along with her own, grabbed her daughter's hand, and led her toward the exit as fast as she could without running.

14

W hile Xander waited for his family to come back out from the supermarket, he climbed from the back seat to the front. *Now, let's see if there's any good music on*, he thought, smiling to himself. With Kala around, it was a rare day that he got to sit up front. He enjoyed the way being up front made him feel—like he was more grown up— responsible, not some *little kid* who was too small to do anything.

Xander was pleased with himself, being trusted to be all alone, even if it was for just a few minutes. He looked at the set of keys in his hands. *Dad really left me with these*, he thought, understanding how important a privilege it was.

He looked through the windshield, watching for his family to exit through the store's sliding doors. He checked the time, thought, *Dad's probably not even close to being done*, then turned to look out across the parking lot. A group of boys, a little older than Kala, caught his attention. *What are they doing over there?* Xander thought, watching them near the edge of the pavement, in the shadow of a grove of pine trees. It looked like they all had sticks—poking at something.

One of them looked up, noticing him watching. Xander looked away fast, cheeks flooding with color at being caught staring. He tried to make himself busy, but there was not much he could do other than fiddle with the radio again. *I wish I had a phone to look at, like Kala*, he thought, wishing for the thousandth time he was old enough to have the same things as her.

There was a knock on the window. Xander looked over to see one of the boys from the group staring at him. "Hi," he called through the glass.

The boy outside motioned for Xander to roll down the window.

Xander shook his head no.

"You scared?" the boy asked through the glass.

"No."

"Then roll it down."

"Why?"

"Chicken."

Xander didn't reply. He sat there feeling like his face was on fire, wishing he had something clever to say to the older boy, but he was too shocked by the interaction to think of anything worth saying.

The boy started to turn and walk back to the others.

"Wait," Xander called. He pressed the button to roll down the window.

The boy smiled at Xander, looking pleasantly

surprised. When the window was all the way down, he raised the stick he'd been holding to Xander's eye level —and that's when he saw the spider.

Xander's eyes virtually bulged out of his skull when he saw the little black spider crawling on the end of the stick. He screamed so loud the other boy nearly dropped the stick on top of himself. "Get that away from me!" Xander cried, reaching for the window button again. He pulled it, but the window was too slow. He pulled harder, frantically trying to get it to go faster as the other boy slowly pushed the stick toward him, grinning like the Cheshire cat.

Xander screamed again, even louder. The car shut off—the window stopped rolling up. He backed his way across the center console to the driver's seat, where he turned the key to accessory, bringing the battery back on. The stick was inside the car now—the spider loosely hanging on to the edge of it with its little legs.

The window is too slow! Xander thought, eyes brimming with tears as he watched it near the top of the door. At the rate it was moving, it seemed it would take an hour to close all the way. He imagined what the spider would do to him once it climbed off the stick— the pain it would cause.

His eyes landed on the full bottle of water in the cup holder. Without thinking, he twisted the cap off and threw the entire bottle at the teen, squeezing it at his eyes with a vicious scream. The boy was taken off guard, stumbling backward, choking on the liquid. He held on to the stick, pulling it outside the car as he fumbled.

Xander rolled the window up the rest of the way

and hit the lock button on the door just to make sure. He scanned the roof, passenger seat, floor—anywhere the spider might've fallen. *Where is it? Where is it?* he thought, holding out hope that it didn't fall off the stick while it was inside.

From the corner of his eye, the boy outside appeared to be choking. Xander watched him carefully through the glass, gagging and clawing at his throat. *Oh my god, he swallowed it!* He held a hand against his own neck. And as terrible as the thought was, he had another greater one—*At least it's not in here.*

Tears were running down the older boy's cheeks as he twisted and convulsed on the pavement. His group of friends ran over to help him—a few picked him up from the ground, a few more banged against the truck. Palms slapped against the hood and windows, then Xander heard a scraping noise against the door and knew they'd cut into the paint with something. *Mom and Dad are gonna kill me for this,* he thought, too afraid to do anything but watch in terror at the group of boys outside.

A muffled scream came from a distance. Other figures were running toward the truck—the boys outside saw them first, held their friend, who was still choking on the spider and ran for the trees. Xander turned again to see his mom and sister coming through the store's sliding doors, yelling at the boys.

Thank God, Xander thought, climbing back into the back seat. Already on the verge of tears, the dam broke when his mom opened the door and cried, "Where's Dad?"

"He had to poop!" Xander screamed, swiping at his wet cheeks.

"How long has he been gone?" she asked, sharing a look with Kala.

"I'm not sure, I lost track of time. A few minutes."

"How the hell did you lose track of time?" Kala said.

"I just did. Okay?"

"We need to get the hell out of here," she said.

Xander threw up his arms. "I'm not the one pooping! Go get him if you're in such a hurry."

Kala flushed. Her hands tightened on the seat as she prepared to unleash her fury. Then their mom cried, "Look, there he is!"

He was holding his stomach with one hand, looking to be in a great deal of pain. The argument was forgotten as all three sets of eyes watched Hart, drained of all color, struggle to walk upright across the parking lot.

"What's wrong with him?" Xander whispered.

Ivey sighed. "It's called irritable bowel syndrome. You know your dad has problems with—"

"No—he doesn't look normal."

She looked at Hart again, still trying to make his way to the car, releasing another sigh. "I better drive." She got out, walked around to the driver's seat, and started the car, all while he was still trying to make it to them.

Ivey honked the horn, waving at Hart through the windshield. "Hart! Come on!" she cried.

A few seconds later, he was there, wiping the sweat from his brow as he climbed into Ivey's vacated seat. "I'm sorry. Not feeling so hot," he said.

"Hart, we have to leave. Those spiders are here. We have to go!" She took off back toward the motel.

"They're *here?* How do you know?"

"Kala saw one in the produce section."

"Jesus." He looked down at his hands in his lap. "Was it from us, you think?"

"No. We've been careful."

"I saw one too," Xander said, speaking up.

Ivey looked at him through the rearview mirror. "Why didn't you say anything?"

"Where was it?" Hart said.

"Some teenagers were messing with it outside."

"We have to leave this place. We have to, Hart!" Ivey cried. She weaved in and out of traffic, honking and swerving, desperate to get them back to the motel as fast as possible.

"What about the police?" Hart asked, halfway groaning as the car swerved, making his stomach even more upset. "What about our jobs, the kids' school—"

"Forget the police! Forget it all! Those fucking things are here! Don't you get it?"

"Okay. Okay, you're right. We need to get the hell gone."

THEY PULLED into the motel parking lot, found their room, and started to pack up what little belongings they had with them. Hart struggled to maintain composure through the pain in his stomach and bowels, but he did what needed to be done. They were going to have a long drive ahead of them before they could stop again, and he wanted to make sure Ivey and the kids had everything they needed because once he sat back down, he wasn't getting up again—unless it was to take another shit.

15

The pest guy got the text from his receptionist almost immediately.

> Emergency in town. Owner at the supermarket says it's life and death.

> I'll have to cancel on Rafe Roberts. Is it worth it?

> He knows everyone in town. You tell me.

Warren sighed, understanding that this—pest control—would now be a political issue. *People can't stand to wait their turn in line*, he thought, fed up with the popularity contest in this town. It seemed to Warren that the more people you knew here in Rock Creek—and the more that liked you, the more likely you were to get your way with anything—even something so mundane as pest control.

He knew what he *wanted* to do, and he also understood what he *had* to do. If he wanted to stay in business, he couldn't piss off the guy who held the most sway in town. It was as simple as that, no matter how unfair or annoying it was.

> Alright. I'll wrap up and head over there. Give me 20.

Warren started to pack his equipment in the truck when another reply came through.

> He says make it 15. You want me to call Roberts?

Warren slammed his fist against the side of the truck. *I should tell him to go to hell.* It was another thing he wanted to do but wouldn't for the sake of business.

> I'll handle it

He made the call that he didn't want to make. "Hey Rafe, I'm so sorry to do this but there's been an emergency and I need to postpone our appointment."

Rafe was silent on the other end of the line for a moment before asking, "When do you think you can make it out? These spiders are getting kind of ballsy around here if you know what I mean."

"I can be out the same time tomorrow. I just have to take care of this today, then you're the first on my list."

Another pause, then Rafe said, "Okay, not a problem." He didn't mention the padding he agreed to pay to get an early appointment.

"I appreciate your understanding. Believe me, if I didn't have to do this, I wouldn't."

"No worries. I know how it goes."

The call ended, and Warren finished gathering his equipment.

Fifteen minutes later, he pulled up to the back of the supermarket. Warren knew better than to go through the front door—businesses usually liked him to keep a low profile in situations like these. *I really shouldn't care what they want today, they're damned lucky I'm even here*, he reminded himself as he searched for the owner's office. Asking nicely was one thing—demanding and expecting was another.

Luckily, he didn't have to go very far. Within a few seconds of entering the building, despite his attempts at keeping himself relatively unnoticed, Warren was bombarded with people asking him questions, pointing to the back of the store, and others calling through the aisles to the boss himself, eager to overhear the conversation with the pest guy and find out exactly what the hell was going on. The owner approached with a grim expression, hissing, "About time you showed up."

Warren's hackles went up. "I have other customers. I had to cancel on one just to get over here now."

"They're not as important as *this*," the owner sneered.

"They probably feel a little different about that."

The owner looked Warren up and down with a grimace. "Who's this other customer who's so important? Who's more important than providing *food* to an entire community? Who could possibly be so important that not helping them is such an inconvenience?"

"That's not what I meant at all. Please, it doesn't matter now. I'm here. What's the problem?"

The owner's eyebrows shot to his hairline. "The problem? The problem is, I have customers leaving this store, crying bloody murder over some *pests* that got in here. I didn't see any of them, but apparently everyone else in produce *has*. I need this dealt with swiftly and discreetly."

"I'll do my best, but I'm not sure how discreet it's really going to be if people see me over there doing what I need to do. You may want to close the store for an hour."

The owner's lips pressed together in a fine line. His bushy eyebrows dove down, almost entirely covering his eyes. "You want me to do WHAT?"

"I just meant—"

"Why don't you let me worry about my own business? Your job is to take care of the bugs."

Warren nodded, not in the mood to stand here and chat with this friendly gentleman any longer. "Which way, sir?"

The owner led him down the back main aisle of the store until he came to the produce section. "Apparently they're near the apples," he said, then walked away, leaving Warren to handle the situation.

THE FIRST THING Warren had to do was find the source of the problem. The pests were seen on the apples, so that's where he went first, knowing very well it could be something that just hitched a ride on the top of someone's shoe, or maybe it had been in the apple crate from the time it was picked at the farm. An infestation was *not* likely, but Warren would do what he needed to do to satisfy the owner. A little extra spraying around the place never hurt anyone.

"Warren? Is that you?"

Warren jumped at the shrill voice he knew so well. He kept searching in and around the apples, trying to ignore her.

"Warren Bailey?"

She was on him now—he could ignore her no longer. Reluctantly, Warren turned to see his neighbor staring at him. "Hi Jewell," he said, plastering a fake smile on.

"What on earth are you doing?"

"I'm here on a job."

She frowned at the apple in his hand while scratching behind her ear. "Are the bugs here, too?"

"I haven't seen one yet, but that's what I'm here to find out."

"I heard the girl crying about spiders, screaming nonsense about a cave and needing more light."

Warren nodded noncommittally. He was only half

listening, trying to get on with the job at hand so he could get back to his real customers.

"I suppose they *made an appointment*," Jewell muttered under her breath.

"Well, it's nice seeing you, neighbor. I'll just get back to it, then." Warren started to turn, but Jewell stopped him.

"Wait—Warren, this is serious."

"What is it?"

"I really need you to spray my house. It might be worse than that. I think—I think I have some kind of infestation." She'd moved from scratching behind her ear to scratching the top of her scalp.

Here we go again, Warren thought. "I'd love to help, Jewell. Just call the office and set something up. Like I told you before, I'm pretty slammed lately and I need you to get on the books so I can have time carved out for you."

"I don't have *time* to do all that," she cried. "I need this taken care of right away, Warren."

He sighed. "Unfortunately, that's how everyone feels."

"It's just not right. It's not right that you won't take care of your neighbor," she cried again, her voice steadily growing louder. People were already eyeing Warren sideways, now they were staring shamelessly.

"Can we keep our voices down?" he said, lowering his own, his face turning red.

"No. I will not lower my voice. I demand to be treated with respect!" Jewell had both her hands weaved into her hair now, scratching herself with abandon.

"I do respect you, Jewell. You have to understand—"

"Oh, I understand alright. I understand perfectly. You're discriminating against me!"

Warren's eyes went wide. "I'm *what*? Jewell, that's a serious allegation—"

"You're refusing to help me because I'm elderly."

"I couldn't care less about that! What on earth are you talking about?" he hissed. "If this is an attempt to publicly embarrass me, congratulations, you win." He threw up his hands. "I'm finished with this conversation, Jewell. I'll see you around."

Warren didn't even want to think about how many people had heard and *believed* Jewell's outburst—the repercussions for his business if a rumor like that got out—a one-hundred-percent *false* rumor—this could turn into a nightmare quickly. He reached to put the apple he was still holding back onto the stack of other apples, then moved to the other side of the produce section to get away from Jewell.

Jewell stared after Warren for a moment, rubbing a hand against her temple, still frowning. "This isn't over," she said before turning to leave.

16

The group of teens in the supermarket parking lot watched the family in the truck drive away like a bat flying out of hell. They watched customer after customer leaving the store with disgusted looks on their faces and no bags in hand. And they continued to watch when, a few minutes later, the pest guy showed up.

"What do you think is going on in there?" Dylan asked.

"Maybe someone else swallowed a spider," Jamie snickered.

Hollis elbowed him in the gut. "That's not funny. That shit was nasty as hell."

Jamie held his stomach, half choking, half laughing. "Oh yes, it was! You shoulda seen the look on your face!" He doubled over in a fit of giggles, some of the others doing the same.

"You're all assholes," Hollis complained, his face scarlet. It wasn't his first time ingesting some kind of creature—he'd even eaten a slug as a dare—but there was something about this one that didn't sit right with him. *It's like it clawed at my throat the whole way down*, he thought, remembering the horrible feeling. He didn't think spiders could do something like that.

"Look, there're more!" Dylan cried, pointing at something.

The group moved farther into the shadows to see the trail of tiny black spiders tucked up in the shadows.

"Where do you think they're going?"

"To their web. Duh."

"I don't see a web. Do you, genius?"

The three of them followed the spiders farther into the trees. There were plenty of spiderwebs around, but these spiders didn't seem interested in them. They looked like they were on a different kind of mission.

"How far are we going to go?" Dylan asked.

"Don't you want to see where they're headed?" Jamie said.

They kept going farther and farther—into the trees, away from civilization, until the trail of spiders they'd been following disappeared. The forest was already dark from the thick trees blocking out any sun, and it was growing darker by the minute because of the time of day. "Did you hear that?" Hollis hissed, jumping.

"I didn't hear anything," Jamie said.

"There!" he cried, pointing into the dark.

They all heard it now. Something moving through the pine needles. Each of them strained to listen or see what was out there.

"Listen," Dylan whispered.

"What is it?" Hollis whispered back.

"There's no sound at all."

Three sets of terrified eyes met. "Let's go back—" Jamie started.

"No. I want to know what's going on. Come on, let's keep going."

"But we don't know which way we're heading."

"It doesn't matter. We'll come across spiders eventually—it's the forest!"

Dylan was the unnamed leader, so the others followed just like he wanted. The quiet of the forest stretched around them like an itchy blanket, making all of them scratch and twitch with nerves. They wanted it gone, wanted the sounds of owls and mice and crickets and all the creatures.

"It's getting dark," Hollis said. "Any of you have a flashlight?"

"Use your phone," Dylan said, bringing out his own.

With the three beams of light on, a sound finally came, and it was near. A skittering—something large. A moth flew past Dylan. He reached out to catch it as it circled back toward the light. "Watch this," he said, holding it by its wings.

A few feet away, he spotted a large spiderweb in a tree, spanning between the trunk and lowest limb. Carefully, he placed the moth onto the web and then stood back to watch.

"That's cold, bro," Jamie said.

"Just watch."

"Are you sure about this?" Hollis asked. "That web looks kind of big…"

"Wow, both of you are pussies today, I swear!"

They watched the moth struggle and fail to free itself against the sticky web. A moment later, there was movement from the spider. It inched its way toward its free meal before digging its fangs in. The moth twitched as venom pumped into its body. Then the spider wrapped it up—a meal best kept preserved for later.

"Spiders are fucking vicious," Hollis said, grimacing.

"That's why they're so badass," Dylan said.

Before the group could walk on, another figure appeared. There was a collective gasp as another spider —this one the size of a small cat—lowered itself above the other spider and its web.

"Holy shit, it's a cannibal," Dylan said.

"Why is it so *big*," Hollis said. "Are spiders supposed to be that big?"

None of them had ever seen a spider so massive, so utterly frightening. They watched, fascinated and horrified, as the giant creature devoured the smaller one of its own with seemingly no effort at all, then turned its eight coal-black eyes on them.

"We should get out of here," Jamie whispered. "Call me a pussy all you want, Dylan, I'm out." he took a step backward.

"Wait—" Dylan started, but Jamie ignored him, leaving with his third beam of light.

The forest around them grew dimmer, even with Hollis being mere feet away. The spider inched toward Dylan and Jamie, who were still staring gape-mouthed at it. They didn't need more incentive to join Hollis. As one, they ran to catch up with him, but they saw with dismay that the spider followed too.

"What do we do?" Jamie asked.

"It's not going to hurt us—it's a spider," Dylan said.

"Uh, spiders can be fucking mean, in case you haven't noticed."

"And did you miss the size of that thing?" Hollis chimed in. "It could eat us for dinner if it felt like it."

"Don't be stupid. There's no way that would happen."

"OK, like I said before, what do we do?" Jamie said. "I'm not going to let that thing follow me home. My little sister is still a baby. She'd be helpless if it got in the house."

The three boys glanced behind them again. The spider was still behind, sticking to the shadows, but it was closer now than ever. "We need to lose it," Hollis said. "Jamie, keep your light shined toward it so we can keep an eye on it. If it gets closer, we'll have to run."

Jamie did as he was asked. When he did—the spider fell farther back until the gap between them was so great they couldn't tell where it was. Dylan's eyebrows raised. "You guys... what if we trap it?"

The group stopped walking. "Are you serious?" Hollis asked.

"You bet your balls I am. Who's going to believe us when we tell them? What if it's some kind of world-record-sized spider?"

"Here in Rock Creek?" The sarcasm dripped from Jamie.

"Yes! There's the old condemned cave a few miles out—in fact, I bet that's where the thing came from."

"But why would it come down here now?"

"Who the hell knows? It doesn't matter. What matters is—we need to capture it while we have the chance. Besides, what's keeping it from going into town on its own? It doesn't need us to show it the way." Dylan looked into Jamie's eyes. "Think about your baby sister."

Jamie nodded. "Okay. I'm in."

THE MEMORY of their Cub Scout days from long ago came back to each of the teens. The plan was simple: set up a snare trap and lure the spider into it. Once they had it trapped, Dylan and Jamie would stay to keep an eye on it while Hollis ran for help.

There was no way to transport the creature—it was far too big for them to carry, even if they did it together —*if they dared, which they didn't*. It was a good plan. The only thing they needed was wire or rope for the snare.

Jamie looked down at his wrist, where he wore a survival bracelet his mom had given him for his birthday. He took it off and held it out to Dylan. "It's made out of parachute cord."

"It's perfect," Dylan said with a grin.

The three of them started when they heard crunching leaves behind them. For a moment, their three minds shared a single thought: *It's here. It's come to get us.*

But it wasn't the spider.

A dark-gray house cat with large yellow eyes appeared. It stopped to claw at the base of a tree, kneading its nails into the bark. Then it meowed at them as it continued on its way, without a single care in the world.

The boys looked at each other. "What the hell?" Dylan said.

"Should we try to stop it? The spider—" Hollis started.

"I've seen that cat before," Jamie said. "It looks like that lady's cat from in town. It's always in her front window when I ride my bike to school—I think his name is Shadow."

"There could be a hundred cats that look like that one," Dylan said.

"It doesn't matter. It's in danger out here," Hollis said.

"No. We stick to the plan. Besides, it's gone anyway." Dylan pointed in the direction the cat left. It was nowhere to be seen now, almost like it had disappeared.

"Be careful, cat," Hollis called into the void of the forest.

THE SNARE WAS SET. The bait—Hollis, waiting alone in the dark—was set. Dylan and Jamie were in place. Now, they just had to wait.

It didn't take long.

Within a few seconds of the halo of light leaving

Hollis, the spider made itself known. Hollis sat shaking, on the verge of losing his bladder, as the giant arachnid crept upon him. He clenched his eyes shut tight, unable to bear looking. If something went wrong—if he died, he didn't want to see it coming for him.

Then a shriek filled the air as the spider's leg caught in the snare. Hollis's eyes flew open to see the spider struggling against the paracord that was now knotted around it. Dylan and Jamie rushed forward. "Are you okay?" they asked in unison.

Hollis nodded, unable to speak.

"Okay, we'll stand watch. You go get—" Dylan started. He stopped—because the spider was ripping its body away from its own leg to free itself. With a final pull, the spider was no longer trapped. It came forward, training its eyes back on the boys.

"Run," Dylan said.

He didn't have to repeat himself. Jamie and Hollis ran. The group flew through the woods as fast as they could, and in the process, they became disoriented. The darkening surroundings, coupled with the unfamiliar forest—they were out farther than they normally went by now—and the panic that blinded them only served to create more confusion.

By the time they stopped to catch their breath, they were as good as lost.

"Look!" Jamie called. "There's the cave up ahead."

"Are you crazy? That's probably where the thing lives!" Dylan cried.

"What if it's not? Or what if it left for a reason and doesn't want to come back?"

"What if! What if! What if we go in and never come back out?" Hollis cried, fully in agreement with Dylan.

"Alright." Jamie threw up his hands in defeat. "Where do we go? What do we do now?"

The other two considered. It was much darker now... and they were lost. They might've lost the monster for now, but for how long? Was it still hunting them? And, most importantly... was the cave really that dangerous?

"It doesn't like the light," Dylan finally said.

The others nodded.

"If we go in there, we can stay by the entrance. We can take turns preserving our batteries until we can think of something else."

"Are we going to be out here all night?" Hollis asked.

"God, I hope not," Jamie said.

"Are we doing this or what?" Dylan asked, avoiding the question.

They were in agreement. It was the only option as far as any of them saw. They were too afraid of becoming even more lost than they already were, especially with the spider lurking in the night. Maybe it would find some other prey to feed on this night and forget all about the boys who huddled together, freezing, afraid for their lives.

17

J ewell came home from the grocery store angrier than ever. The *nerve* of Warren to get into a public argument with her like that—to call her *old*, to make her feel helpless—was even worse than before. It was unforgivable.

Didn't he understand that she didn't have the time or energy to call and book an appointment? He was her neighbor, for crying out loud! She'd told him time and time again and still couldn't wrap her mind around his reasoning. Jewell knew damned well he made exceptions—everyone did. She just wasn't important enough to be on the receiving end of one.

"He's getting too big for his britches, is what the problem is," Jewell said, walking through her front door. "He runs that business of his and now he thinks he's a hotshot. Isn't that right, Shadow?" She scratched her head, driving her long fingernails into the roots of her hair. Nothing she did—no amount of scratching would satisfy this urge to itch herself. She looked for her cat, who normally greeted her when she came home and who was so willing to listen to her complain about the day's goings-on.

He wasn't on his usual perch near the window nor on the couch wrapped up in the throw. Jewell moved to the bedroom, but he wasn't there either. "Shadow?" she called again, growing worried.

Maybe he found whatever's in the ceiling—no, maybe not because that would mean it got out somehow... Jewell paused to scratch her scalp again. As she did, she squinted, trying to focus on the sound coming to her ears. It was faint—just out of reach of recognition.

"What are you?" she whispered. It seemed like—*no, it can't possibly be*, she thought, banishing the idea that the sound was coming from *inside* her.

The sound stopped. Then a different sound came— one she recognized well. It was the sound in the ceiling above her.

Jewell rushed to the wall, slapping her palm against it several times. "You leave me the hell alone!" she cried.

Her head began to itch again. Jewell groaned at the irritation, driving her fingernails once more into her tender flesh. When they came away, there were strands of hair in them. A bald spot was starting, she was sure. Anger bubbled up inside her. She felt like a volcano ready to erupt at any moment, only she wished she could spew her lava at her dear neighbor *Warren*.

"Poor Shadow, I'm not going to erupt at you," Jewell called, still searching for him. As she walked through the house, she made sure the lights were all on. They still seemed to help with the noises—if not completely, at least some.

Eventually, Jewell gave up her search for her cat, who she assumed was asleep in some corner, or just ignoring her like he often did. She made her way to the kitchen to heat up some dinner before settling down on the sofa to watch her favorite show.

She stared down at the chicken on her plate. There was something about it—something she couldn't quite put her finger on. *Maybe I'm just hungrier than normal*, she told herself, sucking in the saliva that was filling her mouth.

She was on the verge of drooling over the meat. It looked better than she remembered from two nights ago. Leftovers were not typically that appetizing, but *this* looked heavenly. It smelled divine too. Jewell almost couldn't hold herself back, but she refused to eat like an animal, no matter how much she wanted that chicken in her belly.

A voice inside Jewell's mind cried out, *meat! Eat the meat! More meat!* She looked at it no longer because she was too busy ripping into it with her teeth.

GREASE from the chicken was smeared over Jewell's face and hands. She lay back against the couch, content even if just for a while. Her eyes grew heavy as she watched the TV. The lack of sleep was getting to her, she knew.

A buzzing noise came to her. She forced her eyes open to reach for the remote. Jewell muted the TV, but the buzzing was still there. She turned the TV off, but it did nothing to stop the sound.

Wide awake now, Jewell turned her head to look across the room. *There's nothing else on,* she thought, dismayed. She slapped a hand against her forehead in frustration.

The buzzing stopped.

Jewell's eyes widened in alarm.

The buzzing came back.

No... it can't be, she thought. But even though she didn't understand it, couldn't believe that it was possibly true, she slapped herself on the forehead again—a little harder this time.

The buzzing stopped once more.

"Holy crap," Jewell said.

The itching came back worse than ever. Jewell dug all ten of her greasy fingers into her scalp to scratch and tear away at her skin. She looked at them as she pulled them away—blood was on a couple of her fingertips. "Is this what you wanted, Warren? You wanted to see me go crazy in my own home, didn't you? I should march over there and show you just how crazy you've made me!"

She pulled at her right earlobe. The itching was inside her ear now, deep within her ear canal.

Jewell drove a finger inside to scratch around, but it did nothing to ease the sensation. She looked at the TV tray beside her, still holding her dishes and silverware from dinner. Her eyes landed on the fork first. *No, won't fit.* Then her eyes drifted to the knife.

She winced. *A steak knife, Jewell, come on, you're going to do some damage, woman,* she told herself. But she couldn't draw her eyes away from it. All she could see was the size of the tip. It would fit. She could inch it in... not too far... carefully... it would work. She was sure of it.

The itch intensified so much Jewell's eyes began to water. She clawed at her ear, desperate to find relief, but it did no good. At a point where she could no longer focus—could no longer stand the feeling—she reached for the steak knife, bringing it up to and *inside* her ear canal.

The tip of the blade entered. She twisted gently, scraping around the channel carefully... but it wasn't enough. She pushed a little farther, twisting a little harder, now slicing into skin.

Jewell felt the blood trickling down to her earlobe, knew she was hurting herself, but couldn't stop. Not yet. She was so close...

The tip of the knife penetrated something within her, bringing untold relief and pain. She brought the blade out fast, reacting to the sudden pop. As she did, the entire inside of her ear canal was sliced open.

Blood filled the space, flowing freely out and dripping onto her shoulder. The knife dropped to the couch. Jewell held a hand to her ear, understanding she'd done something terrible to herself but also understanding that whatever she did—the itching was gone. That's what mattered most.

PART VI

18

Rafe wondered what on earth kind of emergency could be going on for the pest guy to cancel on him last minute. *A pest control emergency must be a big deal,* he thought. Then he imagined all the other jobs that needed doing around the house and realized maybe this wasn't such a bad thing. He remembered his handyman—the one who was always willing to work for cash on short notice. *I'll have him out while I wait for the pest guy to reschedule. He can do a few things in the attic,* Rafe thought with a burst of energy.

IT DIDN'T TAKE LONG for his handyman to show up. Just like Rafe imagined, the man was eager for work—and for cash. Within a couple of hours, he pulled up the driveway in his beat-up truck, ready to get to it.

"Thanks for showing up so fast," Rafe said, shaking the man's hand.

"My pleasure, boss. You know things are tight right now."

Rafe nodded his understanding. "I'm glad to have your help, especially with my leg taking me out of the game."

"Sorry to see you're hurt. Is it bad?"

"Nah. Doc says it's not broken, just a little busted. Anyway, hope you're not afraid of the dark because that's one of the things I need you to fix up there."

"I love the dark. Dark is my middle name."

"Good. Let me show you the way up there." Rafe handed his crutch to Frank to carry while he stuck a flashlight in his back pocket and swooped down to pick up his dog. He leaned heavily against the banister on the way up to the second floor. From there, he took it back to lead the way down the hall to what looked like an old closet door. He then handed the crutch over one last time for the final ascent into the attic.

At the top of the narrow staircase, Rafe twisted the handle of another door, but this one wouldn't budge. Boo whimpered in his arm. He gave a sheepish smile to his handyman. "The first item on your fix-it list."

"Easy peasy. Want me to open it?"

Rafe gave the door one more shove, and it flew open. Both men's nostrils flared at the musky scent that assaulted them. "Can you guess item number two?" Rafe said.

"There might be a leak," Frank answered, following him through the doorway.

Rafe flipped on his flashlight. "There is. The window over there is broken. I had it duct-taped, but as you can see, that hasn't held up very well." he shined the light over the broken window.

Boo shifted in his arms.

Looking at her, Rafe asked, "You want down, girl?"

She only stared at him with large brown eyes, panting her contentment. She didn't indicate that she wanted down and Rafe didn't feel like trying to bend over again without the crutch, so he kept her how she was. To Frank, he said, "Number three—well, four, I guess if you count the window—there are no lights. I don't know if it's bad wiring or just a bulb out, but I'm going to leave it up to you to find out."

"Keep 'em coming."

"The major thing—at least what I've come across so far—is the wood rot." Rafe shined the flashlight around, pointing to the spots he knew of. "When you fix the source of the musk—the leak or whatever the hell is going on up here—I'm going to need most of the floor up here replaced."

"It might take me a few days—maybe a week. I can start today, though, that's for sure."

"Take all the time you need. My pest guy is supposed to be coming out tomorrow, but he'll be out of your way." Rafe frowned at all the *things* making the enormous space feel so small and cluttered. "I know there's a lot of crap up here. It's all my uncle's stuff, and well, I haven't had a chance to go through it yet."

"It's okay. I'll work around it as best I can."

"Alright. Let's go back downstairs. I hate it up here."

A few minutes later, they were back on the main floor, discussing pay. It didn't take long—Frank had fair prices and Rafe was willing to pay him what he deserved. Besides, it was either that or wait until his leg healed and who knew how long that would be.

They shook hands. "I'll leave you to it, then," Rafe said. "I'll be outside for a while if you need anything at all."

"I'll just take some quick measurements and I'll be out to grab some things from the truck."

They parted ways, Rafe to take care of what he was able, his dog following at his heels, and the handyman to go back upstairs.

RAFE GRIPPED the weed eater tight, swinging it left and right in a smooth repeating motion. *I can't believe how bad Unc let this place get*, he thought, not for the first time. *I hope he doesn't have a problem working up there with all that shit in the way.* Rafe tried not to let it embarrass him—it was Unc's stuff after all, not his, even if it did legally belong to him.

His crutches lay against the tree behind him, ready to support him if needed. He glanced at them only once so far, glad to be feeling well enough to not need them yet. The weeds were taking over most of the yard, but the areas that couldn't be accessed by the lawn mower were his primary concern.

The part of the yard that extended into the forest looked haggard and overgrown—like anything could be living just on the border, waiting to come invade the house at night. The once landscaped and manicured area—beautiful when Rafe had visited as a child—now resembled something like the yard of an abandoned home from a horror movie. *One more thing he let go*, Rafe thought grimly.

Then he had a better thought. *I'm going to make this place shine again.* He smiled, watching the weeds melt away with every arch of the weed eater. Even if he wasn't going to keep the house and property, he would give it the dignity that it deserved.

Rafe hit a particularly thick patch of weeds, and his string caught. He gave the weed eater some extra gas, trying to yank it free, but the weeds were spun around the trimmer head too tight. The more gas he gave, the more clogged they became until Rafe finally gave up and turned the tool off.

I shoulda just rented a brush hog, he thought, not caring that he couldn't use one because of his leg. His fingers dug into the weeds, ripping them away until the trimmer head was clear again. Then he looked down to see a small black spider crawling over his boot.

As he stood in the shadows of the trees, Rafe considered leaving this job for his handyman too. Frank wasn't a landscaper, but he was cash hungry, and Rafe was sure he wouldn't mind a little minor yard work. He considered the spider, watching it closely. *Where are you going?* he wondered. He soon became fascinated with its behavior—how it walked along the path of the shadows, never going into the light.

Another appeared, and then another, all doing the same thing. *They're going somewhere*, he thought, unable to look away. Before long, there was a trail of tiny black spiders leading into the trees.

Rafe was no longer fascinated. Now he was becoming worried. *Is it normal to have this many of those things all in one spot?* he wondered, afraid to even think the word—*infestation. What if they get into the house? My god—what if they're already inside the house? I saw them by the lamp downstairs—were they the same kind?*

In a burst of anger, he lifted his boot and stomped down on the trail of spiders. He lifted his foot to see the damage. A few had been squished—their exoskeletons and guts were smeared into the grooves of his rubber sole. He lifted his boot again to repeat the slaughter, expecting the nearby spiders to scatter.

His foot came down—he heard the crunch—but none of the others tried to flee. Instead, they all turned *toward* him. Rafe's eyes widened. Then they came forward.

What the hell? he thought, taking a step back. From the corner of his eye, he saw Boo sniffing the ground nearby but still keeping her distance because she didn't like the sound of the weed eater. She looked up at his movement.

"Better stay over there, girl. I don't know what the hell these spiders are thinking." He took another step back. They were swarming now—there had to be a hundred of them, invisible, crawling beneath the dead leaves on the forest floor, beneath all the weeds, all the *things* preventing his view.

Rafe started the weed eater back up. He pulled the trigger to rev the engine. The spiders were still coming. He leaned the head down and squeezed again, annihilating the swarm of spiders and everything else around them.

19

L eft to his own devices and eager to earn his cash, Frank the handyman set to work on the attic. Most of the work required would be replacing old lumber, which would mostly be a piece of cake. The worst part would be the lighting, but that could be a quick fix too, as long as he could see what he was doing to begin with.

Glad Rafe was unlucky enough to bust his leg up or he'd be doing this easy shit himself, he thought, crossing the porch to his truck. He saw Rafe leaning on his good leg, trying to weed whack the yard and smiled to himself at how ridiculous his employer looked. *The man can't just sit this one out, can he?*

He gave Rafe a wave before grabbing a small toolbox from the bed of his truck and heading back into the house. It was the first of several trips back and forth. The handyman whistled to himself as he pulled spare parts and pieces from his pickup and hauled them up past the second story into the attic over and over, in a better mood now than he'd been in days.

Now, what did I do with that shop light? he thought, shuffling through the contents of his back seat. It was the last thing he needed in order to get started, and sadly, something he couldn't do without because of how dark it was up there. He didn't normally keep the portable on him—sometimes his brother borrowed it for his own jobs, but he could've sworn he saw it earlier...

Barking came in the distance.

"Shit!" a sudden yell.

The handyman startled at the sound of Rafe's voice behind him. He turned to see Rafe on the ground, struggling to get up, his little black dog barking and yapping and going crazy.

"Hey, you okay over there?" he called, starting toward Rafe to help him up. Before he took a few steps, Rafe stood, wincing, brushing himself off.

"Fine, just embarrassed," Rafe called back. Scowling, he made his way toward the crutches still leaning against a tree.

"You need me to—"

Rafe waved him off. "Just stay there in case I fall on my ass again."

The handyman waited for him to cross the rest of the yard, his dog still at his heels, until he finally reached the driveway. "That sure is a faithful dog, Rafe."

"She's the best I've ever seen."

"You going to be okay?"

Rafe looked down at his hurt leg. He sighed. "I think I might've made things worse for myself."

"You want me to take you to the hospital?"

"No. No, I'll manage. Thank you, though."

"Hey, you don't have to do this alone."

"It's fine," Rafe said. "You can stay here and keep doing what you need to do." He nodded toward Boo. "Keep an eye on her for me? She'll stay out of your way. She's a good girl."

"Of course. I need to leave for a bit to grab some supplies, but I'll be back within an hour or two."

Rafe sighed again. "I appreciate it. I might be gone a while—I'm not sure how long urgent care will take."

"Hey, no worries. I'll hold the fort down."

"Just lock up on your way out tonight. Don't worry about feeding Boo, she'll be fine until I get back."

"You got it. Now go."

Rafe nodded, then, with effort, climbed into his own truck.

His little dog stood on her hind legs, reaching for his floorboard.

"Sorry, girl, you stay here," Rafe said.

Frank swooped down to pick her up out of the way so Rafe could close his door. He waved as he backed down the driveway. "Just us, girl. I won't bite, promise."

She ignored him, watching her master drive away.

He took her back into the house, where she found her bed to wait for him by the front door. He took a quick look around, wondering if Rafe didn't have his own work light he could use. *Did I already bring the thing inside?* he wondered. For the life of him, he couldn't remember where he put it—he could've sworn he had it with him and not finding it was now driving him crazy.

"I'm just going to run upstairs real quick if you need me, girl," he said to Boo, who continued to ignore him.

As he placed his left hand on the banister, he felt something against the back of it. His first instinct was to wipe it away—so that's what he did. Then he looked at his palm to see a tiny black spider crawling across his skin, heading for his wrist. He brought his hand closer to see it better. As he did, the spider froze—staring back at him with eight unblinking black eyes.

I hate fucking spiders, Frank thought. Then he connected his hands with a quick slap before flicking the spider and its guts off his skin. He continued his way up the staircase in search of the shop light.

USING A FLASHLIGHT, the handyman found his pile of tools in the attic. The portable shop light wasn't here. *Dammit, what a waste of time*, he thought, angry with himself for taking so long to get started. Time was money and he wasn't getting paid by the hour.

The longer he took to get this job going, the less time he had to do other things that needed to be done. If someone else called him with work, he might miss out on the job because most of these people only called him for a fast turnaround time. If he couldn't provide that, he was dead in the water.

Frank started to head back to the door when he

heard a noise across the room. He headed toward the broken window to investigate. *I might have to fix this thing first*, he thought, shivering against the chill. The musky smell was stronger here too—worse than anywhere else, probably because the worst of the rot was over here.

Frank shined his flashlight around the area, looking for the source of the sound. All looked normal. *Must be the draft coming through.*

The flashlight flickered. He smacked the side of it, admonishing himself for not replacing the batteries sooner. These ones had to be getting old.

The same noise came again—a shuffling. Frank spun. The sound was close, but he still couldn't pinpoint it.

He waved his flashlight around. It flickered again. The noise came again too—this time he could've sworn he heard feet—not human feet, either.

"Is that you, Boo?" Frank called toward the door. He expected to hear her pawing or whining to be let in, but she didn't make a sound.

"Alright, Frank, enough screwing around. No more jumping at shadows. Time to get this show on the road." He crossed the area back toward the door, avoiding furniture and other objects that blocked the way. His flashlight flickered again—then completely went out.

Frank realized when the light was gone was when the noise came.

A fast scampering across the wood planks. Another from above. Something hissing.

There's something up here—more than one something,

Frank thought, dread shooting down his spine. The cold hands of fear had their talons in him as he stood in the dark, listening to whatever creature or creatures moved about.

He slapped the side of his flashlight again, but it wasn't turning back on. Frank took a few steps in what he thought was the direction of the door. Something brushed his face—a spiderweb. He swiped at it, accidentally drawing blood with his fingernails.

The hissing came again—louder, *closer.*

Frank rushed the rest of the way to the door. He felt for the handle—found it—twisted. The door was jammed. It wouldn't open.

"Open, you piece of shit!" he cried, kicking at the base of the door.

The creature was close. Frank could feel it. He pounded the flashlight against the door, pulling at the handle with all his might. Something touched his shoulder.

Frank gasped at the contact—then the light came back on. He spun. Staring him in the face was a mammoth black spider, bigger than he was. Hair stuck out from its body in all directions while eight black eyes peered into his soul, ready to devour him whole.

He stood gaping, paralyzed by fear. His brain registered the warm piss running down his leg, but he was helpless to move, even with death staring him in the eyes.

Frank finally found the source of the stench—and the hissing—when the spider bared its fangs at him. It reared back at the light, but Frank only had a split second of hope before the light went out again.

A moment after he was thrown back into pure darkness, Frank felt the spider's fangs drive into his body. He tried to jerk away, tried to scream, to fight, but the venom was faster. It only took seconds for his body to give in. He was still conscious as the spider began to wrap him in a web.

20

Loreen, the Hamilton family's mail lady, found herself in the psychiatric care wing of the hospital, bound to a bed with thick straps around nearly every part of her that was available. She fought against the drugs that were being pumped into her system. It was so tempting to let go—to succumb to the dizziness, the relaxation, the *high*—but she knew she couldn't. She remembered her missing hand. She remembered what was *inside* her.

How long has it been now? How many of them are there now? she wondered, hating to even think of what the answer might be. She pulled against the restraints, testing them, and was barely able to move an inch.

"Hello? I need help in here!" Loreen cried.

One thing she was thankful for—the lights were on. With her dilated pupils, thanks to the drugs, the light was blinding, but it was *on. How do you like that, you fucking parasites?* Loreen thought, wishing they could hear her thoughts from within.

She knew they were in there. She wasn't crazy. No one wanted to listen. No one ever listened! She wished she could just show them one of those little fuckers—just *one* so someone would believe.

No one was responding to her cries.

Loreen looked for one of the little remotes with the button for the nurse, but without being able to move, it was nearly impossible. She wasn't even sure they had one for her in here—if they thought she was too crazy to need one. "Hey!" she called louder, hoping to get someone's attention.

She waited on edge for a response. She tried to keep her mind off the pain—not from half her hand being amputated, but from what was going on *inside*. They were moving around in there, feasting, nesting, doing God only knew what else. It was driving her mad—really mad—as she lay there helpless, forced to listen to them, to feel them within.

She couldn't scratch, couldn't dig, couldn't get them *out*! *How long do they expect me to just lie here and take this?* her mind cried. *They may as well kill me now and get it over with!*

Tears filled her eyes with each passing moment that no one came or responded—each second she felt another spider in her arm crawling deeper through her flesh. Loreen's eyes flicked to the window. The curtains were drawn closed, but she could tell it was dark out. At this time of year, it didn't say much—it could be dinnertime, or it could be the middle of the night. *Maybe they're short-staffed if it's night... maybe there's no one there to hear me, that's why there's no response,* she thought.

But within the next breath, her mind revolted at the idea. *That's bullshit! If they're short-staffed—fine! But why would they leave me without a way to communicate? No—I don't care what their excuses are. Looks like I have someone else to sue on my list of names. By the time I'm done, Rock Creek is going to have my name in its history books!*

"Hel—" Loreen started to cry out again, but a nurse entered, cutting off the plea.

"Hi Loreen. How can I help you, hon?"

Loreen glared at the nurse, who had to be at least fifteen years younger. "I'm not your *hon*. I'm your patient and I'm old enough to be your mother. Show a little respect," she said.

The nurse flushed scarlet. "I'm sorry. Are you alright? I heard you call out."

"It took you long enough. And no, I'm not damned alright!" Loreen tried to raise her cutoff hand and wrist, forgetting she was strapped to the bed. She fought against the restraints halfheartedly, then settled for nodding her head toward her missing appendage. "I'm missing half my goddamned arm and I'm strapped to this bed. How would you be?"

The nurse frowned, still red but slowly gaining composure. "Loreen, when a patient harms themselves the way that you did—"

"I had to get them *out* of me! Don't you get it?"

"That may be. But hurting yourself that way is not okay. We can't allow—"

Loreen was so angry her face was turning purple. "You can't *allow*?" She tightened in a thick, wrinkled purse as she inhaled a deep breath, ready to rip into the poor nurse. "Tell me something. What country are we living in? Did I teleport into China? What happened to *freedom*? What happened to my *rights*? What happened to—" she cut herself off as the nurse approached.

The nurse leaned over Loreen, fluffed her pillows under her head, then reached for the restraints.

I'll be damned, is she actually listening to me? Loreen thought in a split second of elation.

Then the nurse injected something into her IV.

"What did you just—" Loreen shook her head, already feeling foggy. "How dare—"

"It's a sedative. And you'll keep getting it until you're able to calm down. I wouldn't want you to hurt yourself again."

"I'm tied up!" Loreen tried to scream, but it came out as more of a mumble.

"Rest for a few hours, Loreen. I'll check on you soon."

"Wait—"

The nurse left, closing the door behind her. Loreen passed into the black.

SHE WOKE UP GASPING. Something was on her chest, pressing hard, so hard—but it was okay now. She inhaled deeply, again and again, reassuring herself that she could breathe. She looked down as far as she could, seeing nothing on top of her, then she remembered. They were inside.

Something was moving inside her chest now, no

longer in her arm. *Oh my god, they've moved farther in!* Loreen's panicked mind cried. Her eyes bulged as she looked down at herself, watching her skin ripple with the things inside her.

"Nurse! Nurse! Help! Oh my god, help me!" Loreen screamed at the top of her lungs. She kept screaming, but there was no answer. She looked to the window again, saw that it was still dark out, but only briefly wondered how long it'd been since she was drugged. It didn't matter. Nothing mattered except that there were things inside her—and they were getting bigger.

"I need more lights! I need them out!" she screamed. "I need you to get them out! I need more—" She stopped, tilting her head in thought. *Wait a minute... they don't like the light... they crawled back inside me... they don't like the light—they like the dark! Holy hell, I've been doing this wrong from the beginning!* "Nurse! I need my light off! Nurse! Help!" Loreen cried with renewed energy, screaming until her throat was raw.

It didn't matter what she called out or what her plea was, it seemed the nurse wouldn't respond to her if she was panicked. She forced herself to stop crying out, to wait. It was possibly more painful than her body being inhabited. Loreen had no concept of time, no notion of how long the nurse was actually taking other than counting the seconds.

Eventually, the nurse came back. A knock came at the door before it creaked open. The nurse stuck her head inside. "Did you call for me?"

Loreen ground her teeth so hard she thought she might crack her crown. She was *this* close to actually snarling at the woman but somehow held herself back.

"Yes. Would you please turn off my lights?" she asked instead, in the calmest voice she could manage.

The nurse's eyebrows rose. "You want them *off*?"

"Yes."

"I just want to make sure I didn't mishear you."

"You heard me right."

The nurse took a few steps inside the room to get a better look at Loreen. "Can I ask what gave you a change of heart?"

"It's hard to sleep with the lights on. It's hurting my eyes."

"But this whole time you've been begging for them to be on—"

"I want them off!"

The nurse paused at the outburst.

"I'm sorry. Please. You can understand I've had a hell of a day, can't you?"

The nurse nodded. "Yes. That I can, Loreen." She walked back to the door, placed a hand on the light switch, and flipped it off. "Is there anything else I can do?" she asked.

"Will you leave the door open a hair?"

"Sure. I can do that."

"Thanks."

"You bet. Now get some rest." The nurse walked away, leaving Loreen in almost darkness.

I hope it's enough for you assholes—now get the hell out!

TIME PASSED SO SLOWLY Loreen caught herself drifting more than once, even through the movement inside her body. She was itchy everywhere now—her arm, her chest, her stomach, even her hair. The movement was constant now, all the tiny little legs inside her doing whatever the hell they were doing. She kept wishing they would go; they had the chance—the lights were out as dark as they would get. The time was *now,* but they were stalling for some reason.

"What the hell is your problem?" she said to the room, hoping they could understand.

No response came.

Loreen started to drift again when she felt pressure against her lungs, just like before. It was so intense, for a moment, she couldn't breathe, couldn't even exhale, let alone take a new breath. The pressure intensified. Loreen's face flooded with color from the strain. Her mouth gaped open.

Black spots filled the corners of her vision, but just as she thought she would pass out—suffocate and die —the pressure eased slightly. Something was pushing on her from the inside out, using her lungs to get leverage. The skin directly above her sternum had a pulsing bulge that was eating its way through her flesh.

Then it got through.

Loreen screamed in agony as a black mass filled with hundreds upon hundreds of tiny black spiders broke through her chest and into the world. Pressure built in the wound of her arm and soon it was broken open too, allowing more of the creatures to pour out of her. She was a piece of rotted fruit split open, leaking spiders, blood, and gore like a fountain.

They crawled across every inch of her, a plague spreading across the night. But not all of them. Some were still mighty hungry—and there was fresh meat right here. The spiders injected their venom over and over, ready to devour their host turned meal.

A tear slipped from Loreen's eye as she watched her fate unfold. She was losing too much blood, was too far gone to save. She didn't want to be saved because she knew even if they could stop the bleeding, they'd never get all the spiders. Never.

She stayed silent as they covered every inch of her body, as they bit and clawed and wrapped her in a web. As they mated and produced more and more. As they devoured her whole. Until she finally passed into oblivion.

21

The nurse on duty was making her rounds, thinking about how quiet and cooperative Loreen was suddenly being, wondering what had really made her complacent. It could be that the lights made it hard to sleep, sure... but what if she had something else up her sleeve? Loreen didn't strike her as the kind of patient that gave up so easily.

The nurse had dealt with difficult patients before. It was part of the job, came with the territory, and she believed she was a good judge of character by now. She'd had enough patients in her career to know.

There was something haunting about Loreen, though, something different from anyone she'd ever come across. *That she would do that to herself—mutilate her own body*—she shuddered thinking about it. Whatever Loreen believed was inside her, the belief was powerful enough to make her do such a thing.

I should check on her, the nurse thought. She checked the time on her watch, noticed it hadn't been long since her last stop. Something just didn't sit right with her. It was a gut feeling, something was off. She didn't know if it was Loreen's sudden change of attitude or just a look in her eye, but she didn't trust her.

I should've known better than to leave the door open, she told herself, picking up the pace to Loreen's room. *If she somehow got out of the restraints, got out of the room, hurt another patient*—she'd lose her job, maybe even her license. Would she go to jail for negligence that resulted in death? Probably not—but she didn't want to find out.

The nurse turned to head in the direction of Loreen's room. As she approached the darkened doorway, a trail of spiders scuttled across the hallway. She paused at the sight of them coming from Loreen's doorway. "Loreen? Everything okay in there?" she called.

No answer came.

Avoiding the spiders that she knew shouldn't be there, she stepped closer to push the door open. There was movement in the room, along with a wet sound that she didn't like. She reached for the light switch.

Then she screamed.

ACROSS THE HOSPITAL, Rafe waited in a seat outside of urgent care to get his leg looked at once again. The waiting room was crowded—it seemed like every waiting room he ever had to visit was crowded—but things were also moving a little faster than at the emergency room.

He watched the sky darken through the windows as hours passed and his name still wasn't called. Just like the emergency room, priority was given to patients whose condition was more *urgent*, meaning he could potentially keep getting pushed back further down the waiting list as more people entered. Rafe tried to be understanding, but he was also an impatient man. The wait was hard because of the pain and stiffness in his leg and also with the knowledge that he'd left Frank at his house alone.

An alarm went off through the hospital's speakers.

Everyone in the waiting room startled. Sitting up a little straighter, they looked around with wide eyes, wondering what the hell was going on.

Rafe saw police and security rush past, reminding him of the last time he was there. *Jeez, it seems like every time I'm here, they're having some kind of emergency. What the hell could be going on this time?* It brought to memory when he was in the emergency room waiting to be seen. He'd overheard the two nurses then, discussing the patient who mutilated herself and Rafe couldn't help but wonder if this was the same patient. It hadn't been that long ago—*Would they still be here?* he wondered, a little frightened.

Whatever was wrong with that person, whatever made them that crazy to do something like that to themselves—more than once—he sure hoped it wasn't contagious. He'd never heard of an alarm going off like this at a hospital, but he didn't like it. Not one bit.

22

It was late by the time Rafe got home from urgent care. He was surprised to see Frank's truck still in the driveway. A sliver of guilt crept in when he remembered asking Frank to take care of his dog. *I hope he didn't feel obligated to stay,* he thought, making his way inside.

Rafe expected to see Boo in her bed, waiting for him by the door, but when he stepped into the house, she wasn't there. "Boo?" he called, then, "Frank? I'm back."

Neither of them made a response. The house was silent. A little too silent for Rafe's taste. *Boo should be right here, waiting for me, for her dinner.* It made sense he wouldn't hear Frank if he was up in the attic but there was no reason not to hear Boo.

All the lights were out except for the lamp in the living room and the upstairs bedroom, which were both on a timer. Rafe called for his dog again, moving to the living room where she had a second bed, flipping on the rest of the lights as he did.

She was getting on in years—sometimes snored so loud she didn't hear him. "Boo!" Rafe called again, a little louder, when he saw she wasn't in the living room. *Did she actually go upstairs with Frank?* he wondered. It wasn't like her—she was a one-man dog, friendly enough to others, but kept to herself unless it was Rafe. Then he thought, *unless he took her up there to keep an eye on her like I asked.*

He grabbed his flashlight, then moved for the stairs. No one was there to help with his crutches, but he would manage. His dog was somewhere around here, and he didn't like not knowing where. Besides—it was her dinnertime.

Carrying one of his crutches beneath his arm while supporting the rest of his weight against the banister, Rafe made it to the second floor, panting and sweating but in one piece. When he made it to the landing, he wiped his forehead first, then his palms against his jeans. Rafe started to reach for the light switch but noticed the glowing from beneath the bedroom door.

He was struck by a moment of confusion, wondering if maybe Frank lay in his bed. *It's weird, but I mean, it's not like I'm sleeping in it lately with this leg. The couch is my bed now—and if he's watching Boo for me...* he reminded himself. Then he remembered the timer that was connected to the lamp in there.

Rafe saw that the door was closed, too. He made his way to it, pushed it open, and there, curled into herself and shaking like a leaf, was his little dog.

The moment she saw him, she perked up, whimpered, and ran straight for him. She stood on her hind legs, scratching at his pants to be picked up.

"How did you get stuck in here, girl?" he said, moving toward the bed to sit so he could pick her up easier. When he was sitting, he scooped her up and cuddled her close. Boo whined and licked his face like she hadn't seen him in a year.

"What's going on, girl? What's wrong?" It wasn't like her to be so anxious. Seeing her this way made Rafe a little uneasy. "Where's Frank?" he asked more himself than her.

She gave another small whimper and squirmed in his arms.

He shifted her so she was more comfortable, then he left the bedroom, heading for the door to the attic stairs. "I don't know how I'm going to hold you going up those stairs," Rafe said, considering. It was clear his dog was freaked out about something, but he needed his flashlight—there was no light over these steps, and he needed to hold on to the handrail.

His leg was killing him from all this walking and climbing. Rafe knew he shouldn't be on it at all—especially after what the doctor had said today. But how could he just hang out downstairs, not knowing what Frank was up to?

Boo stared at him with her big innocent eyes, waiting for him to make a decision.

"Just a peek to make sure he's okay. I'll be quick," he said, then he set her down and reached for his flashlight that was still in his back pocket. With a pang of guilt, he ignored his dog, who was once again standing on her hind legs, scratching at him to be let up.

Rafe opened the door to the narrow staircase and started his climb to the attic, leaving the door open behind him, in case Boo wanted to follow.

IT WAS WORSE CLIMBING these than the regular stairs— they were narrower, darker, and creepier. As he climbed them, a sinking feeling went straight to Rafe's gut, telling him *something wasn't right there.* He knew if Frank was up there working, he would be making some kind of noise—any kind of noise. But there was nothing other than the sound of his own breathing and Boo's occasional whimper below.

Rafe tried to think of what might've happened to Frank. *He could be asleep, maybe took a little nap, is all. Or —he said he had to get some supplies... maybe he had his brother or an associate with a bigger truck pick him up and he's not even here.* The more he thought about it, the more he believed that's what was going on and he started to feel better. He almost decided to turn back and not even bother with the attic at all, but he was at the door now—*may as well go in*, he thought, placing his flashlight hand on the door handle.

He twisted and pushed, but the door wouldn't open. That's when it hit Rafe that this exact situation might've happened to Frank. *He's stuck in there! That's why he's so quiet—he probably did fall asleep waiting on me to get home!*

"Frank, are you in there?" Rafe called, knocking on the door. He grabbed the handle again, twisted it, and pushed with all his might this time. The door flew open. Rafe came with it, stumbling forward into the dark attic. He dropped the flashlight, trying to save himself from falling. It hit the floor hard, the plastic cracking.

As Rafe stood, catching his breath, he heard movement. "Frank, I'm here now. I got the door open, man. I'm so sorry about that."

Frank said nothing.

"Frank? You in here?" Rafe called again.

Still no response.

Frowning, Rafe bent to pick up the flashlight, groaning at the pain in his leg. He stood—and heard movement again. "Frank?"

Rafe took a few steps in, making sure the door stayed open behind him—he didn't want to wind up stuck in here. He swiveled the flashlight around the area, trying to get an idea of what was making that noise and whether or not Frank was up here asleep. *Whatever's moving around up here, it's big as hell*, Rafe thought, really hoping it was just Frank playing a twisted joke.

He came to the broken window—and stopped dead

in his tracks. Rafe's eyes bulged. He couldn't believe what he was seeing.

In the corner of the attic was a massive spider web, so big it spanned clear across the area, over furniture and anything else that was in the way, almost to the other corner of the attic. There were *things* wrapped in the web—prey that was trapped, waiting to be eaten. Only these prey were big. And one—looked *human*.

"Holy shit," Rafe whispered. He was shocked—stunned. He was paralyzed by fear. Part of Rafe wanted to approach the web to investigate it—confirm if that was actually Frank over there wrapped in a spider's web. The other part of him was screaming at the top of its lungs—*run!*

If that was indeed Frank—something was up here, and it would want him in that web too.

23

R afe took a tentative step toward the web. He hesitated. *I can't leave Frank here like this,* he thought, *but how am I supposed to do anything with this leg of mine? I'll be lucky if the spider doesn't come after me before I can get the hell out of here.*

He took another step, sweat dripping from his forehead into his eyes now. He swiped his arm across his face, using the one holding the flashlight. *Calm down, Rafe, you just need to see—to make sure—then you're gonna get the hell out of here, grab Boo, and call the pest guy on your way to the next state,* he told himself.

His eyes followed the beam of light to the left of the web. A black mass shifted in the dark. Chills ran down Rafe's spine when he heard the hissing. *Holy shit, Rafe, you're in over your head here, buddy.*

Abandoning the idea of getting a closer look at what—who—was probably Frank in the massive web, Rafe took a step backward, keeping his eyes on the mass of black at the edge of the light. *You just fucking stay right there*, he thought, willing his thoughts to go straight to whatever creature was there.

Rafe kept the light focused as he took another step backward. Then he bumped into something. His heel landed against the edge of a piece of furniture, while something on the piece of furniture—a knob of some kind—connected with his Achilles tendon. Rafe cried out in surprise and pain, fumbling forward.

As he faltered, the beam of light from his flashlight moved. He almost dropped it again, once more trying to catch himself before falling on his bad leg. *I'm a goddamned klutz up here!* Rafe thought, angry with himself and the entire situation he found himself in.

The moment he had his footing again, Rafe pointed the light back where he had it—but the black mass was gone. *Shit, shit, shit! Get a move on, Rafe!* Rafe spun back toward the door—and there was the spider.

It hissed at the light, reared up on its back legs, baring its fangs at him. Its front legs curled back in on themselves, and to Rafe, it seemed almost *frightened*. It stood taller than him—so tall it almost brushed the ceiling when it reared back.

For a moment, as with seeing the web, all he could do was stare open mouthed at a creature that seemed—impossible. Then he saw the other movement all around the floor, walls, and even the roof. In the dark—hundreds of those little black spiders were crawling their way toward the big one, staying away from the light, just like it was. They moved as a single unit with one mission. What that mission was—Rafe didn't want to find out.

He kept the light trained on the mammoth, ignored

the pain in his leg, and looked for a way around. It was blocking the way to the door, so he had to go back, farther into the attic, to weave around furniture, hoping it would follow and clear the way to the door. The little ones were more of a concern now—because there were so many and because he couldn't see them.

Rafe turned the flashlight upward, so the light shone like a halo around him. It was a bit dimmer this way, but he felt more protected. His eyes darted everywhere, jumping at every sound. Then he heard the worst sound possible and felt like his heart would stop beating.

Boo's bark. She was up here. And she was barking at the spider.

"No, girl, get out of here!" Rafe cried.

No longer bothering to be careful, he rushed around the rest of the furniture until he had the door in his sight. There she was—his little fifteen-pound black mini pinscher confronting an eight-foot-tall monster. He was so proud of her—wanted to throw his fist in the air, yell, *you get that fucker, girl!* And at the same time, he wanted to cry, to scream, *get the hell out of here, you crazy-ass loyal dog!*

In that moment, seeing her so brave, so willing to fight this demon spider that must've crawled from the depths of hell, Rafe found his own courage. He wasn't about to let anything happen to his uncle's dog—to *his* dog. She was his to protect, just as he was hers. And they were going to make it the hell out of here.

Boo's hackles were raised, so she looked like a little black ball of fluff. Rafe thought he could laugh at how silly she looked if he wasn't scared to death for both their lives. Her bark was small but more ferocious than he'd ever heard. She bared her teeth at the spider, who was baring its own, both of them growling.

The spider brought its front legs down—it looked like it was either trying to step on her or get over her for a better striking position.

Boo dodged and lashed out at one of the legs, giving it a quick, hard bite.

The spider shrieked, bringing another leg down a hair's width from her.

"Run, girl!" Rafe cried. *I have to do something to help her!* he thought, looking around desperately for anything he could use to fight it off or even to throw at it.

Boo continued to bark while the spider continued to attack. She got in another good bite, but from the edge of the darkness, Rafe saw the little ones creeping in. *They're going to blindside her!*

There was no more time to think, to find help, only time to do. He stuck the end of the flashlight in his mouth, holding it with his teeth so he'd have both hands free. Then he picked his crutch up, held it like a bat, and swung with all the strength he possessed. He slammed the crutch down over and over on the spider's back as high as he could reach. Then he brought the crutch lower, trying to hit its legs out from under it, screaming the whole time through his hold on the flashlight.

The spider shrieked at the assault, spun to face him, and was blinded by the beam of light coming from Rafe's mouth. It retreated—away from the light, him, and most importantly—from Boo. The little ones followed suit, but Rafe followed, bloodthirsty now. He swung again at the spider as it fled, screaming through his hold on the flashlight, grinding his teeth around it with the want of the spider's blood.

Rafe jabbed the crutch into the spider's retreating form. For a moment, it stopped, and a little voice inside Rafe's mind urged him, *Don't poke the bear! Get the hell out of here while you can!*

He wished he had a better weapon—a gun, a knife, a goddamn sword... anything to kill this thing—his crutch wasn't going to do anything except piss it off. He didn't want to think how it—*they*—got up here or how long they'd been here while he and Boo lived in ignorance—a few feet from being *eaten.*

He stopped advancing, pulled the light from his mouth, and held it out toward the spider. It did the trick—the spider forgot any idea of turning to fight *or eat* him and kept moving away. Rafe moved in the opposite direction to pick up his dog while he had the chance. Tucking her in close, he held her beneath his arm and walked back through the attic door, locking it behind him.

Then he ran for dear life.

PART VII

24

I t was nearly eight o'clock—hours past closing time, and Warren's phone was still ringing off the hook. It seemed as if the whole town had an infestation, and he was the only one to call, apparently. He didn't want to complain about the amount of business because more business meant more money—which was always a good thing, but he would also like to be home by dinnertime.

The headlights on Warren's truck shone against his garage door as he pulled into the driveway. It was pitch black out—seemed like it was midnight at least, but when he checked the clock on his dash, he saw that it was nowhere near that late.

Sore from a long day of hard work–a long day of dealing with scared, angry people, he declined the incoming call on his cell phone, not caring who it was. He was off for the night, no exceptions. Warren turned his phone completely off, then with a groan, he climbed out of his cab and stepped into the night. As he

came around the front of his truck to cross the driveway, he heard a sound that sent chills up his spine.

"Warren, is that you?" Jewell called from across her
yard.

His *favorite* neighbor was approaching. *How does she
always know when I'm home*, he thought. *And why the
hell does she always feel the need to come over here the
minute I pull into the driveway? I bet she sits there by her
front window and waits for me just so she can come over
here and complain. She better not give me another guilt
trip...*

"Are you just going to stand there ignoring me?" she
said.

Warren squinted into the dark toward Jewel's
approaching form. She looked like she was hobbling,
hunched over, and barely able to make it across the
yard. Something about the way she was walking didn't
sit right with him. Despite her accusations against him,
he didn't believe she was an *old woman* and, in fact,
thought she seemed pretty healthy, all things considered. She was not one to walk like *this*.

There was a voice inside Warren's mind telling him,
Go, just go inside! He felt that old familiar guilt rising up
when he thought about giving her the cold shoulder
and leaving her high and dry there in the night while
he went inside to finally eat dinner.

With a deep sigh, Warren called back to Jewell,
"Good night, Jewell, I am calling it a night." But he
wasn't going to get rid of her that easily.

"Oh no you don't! Wait just a minute, Warren
Bailey! I want to talk to you."

Her shrill voice sent gooseflesh down his arms. *So*

there is something she wants to bitch about. At least she's not going to drop dead on my driveway, he thought. Aloud, he said, "Jewell..."

"No, no. I don't want any of those excuses. Give me just a second to get over there, I'm having a hard time hearing," she said.

The truck's headlights turned off, so Warren moved closer to the garage to kick on the motion lights. They came on, lighting the surrounding area, giving him a good view of Jewell—and giving her one of him.

She held a hand up to her eyes, squinted, and cried, "Turn that damn light off, will you? It's killing my eyes."

He could only stare slack-jawed at what he saw. *That can't be Jewell. I don't know who that person is...* he thought, barely recognizing the person coming toward him with his neighbor's voice. *I just saw her,* he thought, dumbfounded.

As he suspected, she was walking bent over, and he clearly saw that there were bald spots on her head where great gobs of hair were missing. Blood was smeared on the side of her face and ear. "Do you need help?" he called, finally finding his voice again. As soon as the words were out though, he regretted them.

"Help? Of course I need fucking help!" she cried. "What do you think I've been trying to get from you all this time?"

Warren, keep your mouth shut, man! he thought. He raised an arm toward Jewell, who was almost to the bushes bordering their two properties. "I'll see you around," he called, not willing to stand there for a minute longer if he was going to have to listen to it all over again.

To his amazement and horror, Jewell reached the bushes and actually started to climb through them rather than stay on her side or walk around. "Jewell—no. What are you doing?" He started toward her, unsure how to stop her short of calling the police. There were thorns all through them, and though they were small, they could still do some damage.

"I've about had it with you—" she was saying through gritted teeth. She said something else unintelligible, her voice muffled.

"Stop! You're going to hurt yourself!" he yelled, watching her struggle to pull herself free from the brambles.

"It's all your—" She finally yanked herself free and then stood there staring at Warren with cold eyes boring into him. She was panting, trying to catch her breath.

He wasn't sure quite what to say while she collected herself.

The motion light flicked off, leaving them in utter darkness.

"I'll just—" Warren said, moving back into the range of the light. It flashed back on, and Jewell made a moaning noise as if she was in pain.

She started to scratch at herself—dragging her long nails against her bare arms, reaching over and around to get her back, even lifting her shirt to scrape her bare stomach. Then she started in on her head and Warren realized the chunks of hair that were missing—were missing because she was pulling them out.

He reached a shaking arm toward her. "Jewell, stop—"

She let out another deep groan, scratching in a fury now, hardly seeming to notice him standing there at all. "It's... the... light...." she ground out.

Warren looked back toward the garage light, confused. *The light? What the—*

"If you would've just sprayed!" Jewell cried.

Warren flinched as one of her fingernails broke completely off as she dug into her own flesh. Blood poured out of her arm where the broken nail cleaved in.

Then the light flashed off again.

There was a wet ripping sound, a pop, and an agonized scream from deep within Warren's neighbor. He blinked, blinded by the sudden loss of light, then moved another step toward the garage to kick the light on again. Jewell was back in view—but Warren didn't know if he wanted to scream or cry.

She was completely torn open—looked like an egg that had been split, only the shell remaining. Pouring out of her in droves were tiny black spiders, though he could barely make out their color with the blood. They were crawling over every inch of Jewell's skin, across her eyeballs, through her hair, fanning out into the night. Half of them looked like they were trying to curl back up inside her to escape the light, and the other half used those as a shield, still trying to escape into the world.

Holy God, Warren thought.

Jewell collapsed—dead.

Warren moved for his truck before the spiders could get to him. He reached for the back door, where he kept some pesticides. It was locked. *Shit!* his mind cried as he fumbled for the front door to unlock the back. He finally got into the back, grabbed what he needed, and the motion light went out again.

"Goddamn fucking light!" he screamed, swearing on his life that if he survived, he would replace the thing with one that stayed on. He adjusted his sprayer in his sweaty hands, jumping when he felt something brush against his skin.

There was a moment of complete panic, of total hopelessness, when he thought they were on him, thought he was done for, just like Jewell. He'd become a living nest just like her—a sack of flesh for them to mate and feed off of while they multiplied. They'd split him open when he was used up, crawl from deep within his guts, and find some other poor soul to infest.

His jump triggered the light on again—and he saw that there was nothing on him. It was only the edge of the truck door grazing him. *Breathe, Warren! You know what to do here. You handle these bastards for a living!* He knew there was no time to think, to stand there gawking or pissing himself over what they might do to him—no time to consider how unnatural this was or how they were unlike any other spiders he'd ever seen or heard about in his lifetime. There was only time for one thing—spray—kill—as many as he could. *All* of them if he was able.

Warren pulled the spray trigger, coating everything around in the deadly pesticide. When the light eventually shut off again, he waved his arm toward it to kick it back on and kept spraying until the bottle was empty. With each black piece of death that curled up on itself and died, he felt a small surge of relief.

He knew there were some that got away—there had to be. But he was getting all that he could, and for that, he was damned glad. He was glad of his occupation too, and thought, *If I wasn't right here next to my truck, I'd probably be dead meat, just like Jewell. I might still be if they did get me...* he considered looking himself over for bite marks, but there would be time for that later.

The sprayer ran out and Warren moved to the truck to grab more. He coated the entire outside of his truck as a preventive, then backed his way to his front door, spraying the ground and house as he went. He moved inside, locked the door, and kept spraying until all entrance points were covered.

I'll be damned if I get any sleep tonight, he thought. Then he began making a list of all the things he'd need to do to start to get this infestation under control.

25

Morning came. Warren made it through the night, shaking and red-eyed but alive. He'd seen not one of the spiders in his house, but he also kept second-guessing himself, wondering if maybe he actually had fallen asleep.

They could've crawled right up his shoe, then his body, and into his nostril or ear without him blinking an eye. The thought made him itchy and nervous—terrified—to wind up like his neighbor or worse—if there was a worse. Warren examined himself every few minutes to make sure he had no bites or open sores, no sign of their presence. He wasn't sure what he would do if he found one, but he'd think of that if the time came.

Now that the sun was up and lighting the world, he felt safe to go back outside. The first thing he did was open the garage and get to the pesticide. He filled his backpack sprayer with what he hoped was enough to last him, then moved to where Jewell had fallen on the driveway.

She's not here, he thought, seeing blood but no body. *She must be alive... but how?* He thought back to the night before, remembering how she looked with the spiders crawling out of every crevice, creeping over every pore. *No. She was broken—dead. But still... what if I was wrong?*

He was torn, ready to call the police, although he wasn't sure what they would be able to do. Then he considered that in this particular situation, *he* was the one to call to fix the problem. *Fuck!* his mind cried as he realized he was going to have to go into Jewell's house. Either she was there—alive and needed an ambulance, or she wasn't. Either way, he had to find out if there were more of *them.*

WHEN WARREN KNOCKED at the front door, it swung open. "Jewell?" he called, leaning in.

No answer came.

He took a step inside the entryway. "Jewell?"

Still no answer.

He came in the rest of the way, his eyes moving over every inch of the house. There were no signs of foul play, no signs of the spiders or any other pests as far as he could tell. Carefully, he moved into the living room, gripping his spray nozzle tight.

In the living room, he paused when he saw a TV tray with leftovers—and a steak knife covered in blood. He scanned the tray, the couch, the entire room, but there were no spiders he could see. Everything looked normal.

Warren continued through the house, the only thing besides the bloody knife that stood out was that every single light was on. *I should've listened to her. I should've helped her. To hell with an appointment. She was right all along,* Warren thought. Shame filled him with the idea that this was *his* fault. If only he would've cared enough to come check the place out, he might've prevented this before it even started.

He tried again to call out to her before he entered what he believed to be her bedroom. "Jewell? Are you in here? I'm sorry it's taken me so long to help..." He paused, waiting for an answer.

There was a faint noise—something moving or being moved.

"Jewell? I don't want to intrude, but I'm here to help."

Nothing... and then—a noise again—something scuttling, but it wasn't from inside Jewell's room. It was from above.

Warren tilted his head back to look at the ceiling. He strained, trying to hear, but a part of him already knew. *They're up there. That's what she's been hearing this whole time. She tried to tell me,* he thought, as another wave of guilt ran through him. He also realized that there had to be a ton of them up there to make that kind of noise.

Without waiting any longer, he pushed the bedroom door open. It was her bedroom alright. And he found the spiders.

Unlike the rest of the house, there were no lights on

in there. Warren suspected either the breaker had tripped from all the lamps plugged in or, somehow, the spiders had figured out a way to get them unplugged. Either way, the only light now was coming from the hallway.

There were spider webs hanging from all four corners of the ceiling, draped down the walls, and across the furniture. Warren spotted a big hole in the wall behind the bed and suspected it was where they came through. He grimaced, thinking of how they got inside Jewell—*probably in her sleep.*

Without taking a step into the room, he lifted his sprayer nozzle and shot the deadliest pesticide he owned at the creatures. The sound of the shrieking made his stomach roil, but he kept the trigger pulled. Warren stepped into the room, spraying every square inch he could.

The spiders, seeming to notice that *he* was the one responsible, advanced toward him. For a brief moment, Warren's eyes bulged as he watched them swarm almost as one unit toward him. All those tiny black eyes, those terrible little legs, those *fangs*—he considered dropping the sprayer—the entire backpack—and getting the hell out of there.

There would be another way, another chance. He could contact the police for one, and even though they would still need his chemicals, he could get backup. Yes, a second sprayer, or even a third, was just the thing —he took a step back.

An image of Jewell came to mind, cracked open like a shell, an empty husk—her insides *eaten* by those things that were waiting for him to be a chickenshit and run. There was no love lost for the woman—hell, he basically hated her—but she didn't deserve what she got. No one did.

"I hope all you bastards roast in hell," Warren said. He steeled his resolve and took another step in the room toward the swarm. He cranked the sprayer up and let it rip, keeping his ground even when they reached his boots.

Warren screamed a battle cry, thinking of nothing else but raining death upon the vermin. They shriveled up before him but kept coming in droves, climbing over the tops of their fallen comrades in an effort to get to his flesh. Some of them succeeded in crawling up the top of his boots, even reaching his jeans. Warren sprayed them without hesitating, not caring if the deadly chemical was on him—as long as *they* weren't.

Eventually they slowed their approach. He felt a sliver of hope rising—thought, *I might actually make it out of here alive!* Then his sprayer stopped.

Hope was replaced by instant dread, bordering panic. He checked the nozzle, the trigger, the hose—everything was okay. The remaining spiders were gathering their courage quickly—he didn't have long before they'd realize *now* was their chance.

Warren slipped the sprayer pack off his back and set it on the floor before him so he could figure out the problem before it killed him. He fiddled with it, then tried the sprayer again—no luck. "Goddamned thing!" he cried, his voice cracking. He picked it up and slammed it back down, kicked it, then tried the trigger again as a fresh wave of spiders reached his boots.

One more try—he squeezed—and the pesticide

finished off the last of the swarm. Hot tears streamed down Warren's cheeks as he surveyed the room, looking for any survivors. If there were any, they were hiding—possibly still in the walls or ceiling. He could block them off, try to prevent their escape, but realistically would never be able to climb up there and get every single one. It wasn't possible.

"Enjoy your tomb," he said before finally breathing a little easier. He'd emptied almost his entire tank of pesticide—far more than he'd ever need in a normal situation, but this was nowhere near normal. Now that they were no longer swarming or attacking, he could take the necessary steps to seal them in. "I'm not going to let you hurt anyone else. Human meat is off the menu from now on," he said, moving to take care of business.

BY THE TIME Warren was done, he was glad to be out of the house, and even more glad to never set foot in there again. He wished there was a way to have the house condemned, sealed shut and knocked down. *I'll have to see what I can do. Maybe there will be a sudden fire that burns the place down*, he thought.

It was obvious that Jewell wasn't there. She wasn't outside either; her body had moved or *been* moved... but Warren couldn't comprehend what might've happened. He could've sworn she was dead—

They couldn't have eaten her... not that quickly... could

they? It went against everything he knew about the creatures. Although he was no expert, he did know a few things, and that they didn't devour entire human beings without a trace in less than twelve hours was among them. *She was already emptied out,* he reminded himself grimly. But then he thought, *No, it still doesn't add up. Something happened to her body. Something else is out there.*

26

W arren went to check the time and realized
he'd never turned his phone back on
from the night before. He had an
appointment today with Rafe Roberts—he'd put him
off once already, and now he was going to be late
because of this mess. He thought about all the other
clients, the other reports of an increase in spiders this
season. *They're all related*, he thought, knowing it was
the answer.

It made sense. The reason there were so many of
them lately, the reason he was getting so many calls—
the town was being overrun with these things. The only
questions were—who else were they going to explode
out of the way they did Jewell? And—how was he going
to stop them?

Warren turned his phone on, watching all the
missed calls and messages come through. He cringed as
Rafe's name and number came up, hesitating to listen
to the voice mail. It wouldn't be the first time he'd had

an angry client, but it might be one of the few times he regretted it. He liked Rafe—he was a straightforward guy, the job was fair, and the money would be good. He didn't like to upset any client but especially hated to upset one he respected and who was going to pay so well.

Steeling himself, he hit play on the voice mail.

"Warren, hey, it's Rafe Roberts, over at the big white two-story on the outside of town. Anyway—um, I'm not sure how to put this..." Rafe's voice trailed off there. He sounded like he was driving—and he sounded panicked. "There's a big—no, that's not right." He cleared his throat before continuing. "You're going to think I'm nuts, but I swear on my life—there's a *spider,* bigger than I am, in my attic. It tried to *eat* my dog...it *did* eat my handyman. I need to talk to you pronto, man. I need help. I need you to—" The call ended.

Warren was frozen, the same way he'd frozen when he saw the spiders crawling from within his neighbor. Any other time he'd think it was some kind of sick joke, but not today. Today he believed every word from Rafe's mouth. And his tone—his tone told him everything. The man was running for his life and needed his help.

I can't do this, Warren thought. He wasn't ashamed to admit he was frightened. Most people thought he liked bugs and arachnids and all the creepy-crawlies, to be in the profession he was in—but the truth was, he hated spiders just as much as anyone else. He enjoyed finding them and killing them—and *that* was why he was in the profession he was in.

Killing the nest in Jewell's house was one thing, but this—this was a whole different ball game. He didn't want his body to be infested. He didn't want to be eaten by a giant mutant. He didn't want any of this.

Warren closed his eyes tight. Then he slapped himself across the cheek, one and then the next. *Man up, chump. If you don't do it, who the hell will? Some guy from the next town over? By the time he gets out here, they'll all be dead.*

If they continued to spread the way they'd done with Jewell and with her house, there was no question about it. Every resident of Rock Creek was going to be a target for these beasts. And Warren had a feeling that those who the little ones didn't get, the big one would.

This big one that Rafe had found—Warren knew he'd have to face it—to kill it. He was scared shitless, but he didn't have a choice. With a few taps on his phone screen, Warren dialed Rafe back.

Rafe answered on the first ring. "Tell me you don't think I'm nuts."

"I've had my own run-in with the little ones. Trust me, I believe every word of what you said."

"Are you okay?"

"I'm fine. My neighbor—she's not."

There was a pause, then Rafe said, "We have to kill it—the giant one and the little ones too. If we can."

"I'm glad you're willing to help. I won't be able to do it alone."

"It's my house and my dog that almost died. I'm going to make sure the thing is finished."

"Good. We need to meet," Warren said, suddenly not so afraid. He had a partner now, someone to help. It didn't matter that the man probably didn't know a thing about pesticides—what mattered was that he *knew*. He knew what they were dealing with and was prepared to fight it.

"Now?" Rafe asked.

"Yes. Are you at home?"

"Hell no. We left that place as fast as we could."

"Who's we?"

"Me and Boo."

Who the hell is—oh, the dog, of course, Warren thought. After a pause, he said, "I know it's the last place you want to be, but we need to make a plan and if that's where the big one is—that's where we need to go."

"What about your end? You said you had a run-in with the littles."

"I took care of them. There's just one more thing I have to do, then I'll be able to meet," Warren said. He thought again about how he would make sure no one would ever step foot in there again. If someone came along looking for Jewell, they were in for an ugly surprise. *There's no way I got them all...* he reminded himself. No, there was only one solution here. Fire. It looked like that accidental fire was going to happen a lot sooner.

"They almost got me when I was in the front yard. I didn't realize it at the time, but they were this close, Warren." Rafe sounded like a child pleading not to be made to do something.

"Give me an hour, then park on the side of the road at the end of your driveway. Stay in the truck. I'll come with everything I have."

"Okay. Okay, I can do that."

"And Rafe?"

"Yeah?"

"Be ready to fight."

WARREN MOVED to gather what was in his own garage, still keeping his eyes peeled for any little surprise visitors. When he had everything he needed, he made one last trip over to Jewell's. It was still early—most of the neighbors would either be asleep still or just waking up, but he wanted it to burn for as long as possible without the fire department's interference.

Didn't think I'd be back here so soon, he thought, stepping inside with his can of gasoline. He splashed it on every surface of the house, over the walls, even up to the ceiling, until the five gallons were empty. He backed his way to the door, lit the match, and ran.

27

Rafe sat in his truck with his dog, waiting for Warren as instructed. When Warren pulled up, Rafe followed him down the driveway, the whole time questioning his own sanity. *Are we really going back in there? How the hell do we stand a chance against that thing?*

The want for its blood was still fresh on his tongue though, as well as the want for revenge. This thing was in *his* house, almost killed Boo—almost killed *him*. The image of its massive black body was ingrained into his vision, and it would probably stay there even if they managed to kill it. "I don't think we have a choice, Boo, do we, girl?" he said.

His dog, sitting beside him on the bench seat of the truck, only looked at him with her innocent brown eyes, with something that looked like fear.

THE MEN each got out of their trucks, Rafe carrying his dog and Warren his sprayer.

Warren stared at the house for a minute before asking, "Is your handyman still in there?"

"He was when I left."

Warren nodded. "And did you call the police?"

Rafe flushed. "No. I was going to, but I thought— hell, I don't know what I thought, but here I am. I'll call them once the things are dead."

Warren nodded a second time. "Jesus, this goes against everything I've ever known or believed, but I think you made a good call. Now, tell me everything."

Rafe laid out all the details—repeating the information he'd already said on the phone and providing new information like exactly where the web was, how tall the spider was, and how it had attacked Boo.

"Alright. I'll move in first with the spray, but something tells me it's only going to be effective on the littles," Warren said. "We're going to need bigger artillery to get the big one."

"What? Like a gun?"

"You have one?"

"No."

"Didn't think so. A gun might work—maybe—but I was thinking something more along the lines of a flamethrower or a blowtorch. Something to *burn* this fucker."

Rafe couldn't help but smile. He liked the way this man thought. "I don't have any of those things, but maybe we can rig something up. I have a lighter and some lighter fluid. Unc had some old hairspray in the bathroom. I'm not sure what else there is, but I'm sure we can figure it out."

"Good. Let's move. And if we come into contact with the big one before we're ready—if it's downstairs waiting for us—we run like hell. We can always come back."

"Agreed," Rafe said. A shot of pain ran up his leg in protest of the plan. He knew he wouldn't be able to do any running—would be lucky enough to be able to stand without his crutches and not fall down—but he wasn't going to mention it. They had a plan. A good one. And it was going to work.

STILL CARRYING HIS DOG, Rafe unlocked the front door and then stood back for Warren to take the lead.

Warren had his pesticide ready to go, along with the biggest flashlight he owned. He was wearing two head-lamps, one facing forward and down, the other positioned behind him and up to shine at the ceiling. He handed Rafe a spare flashlight and headlamp and took his first steps inside the house.

Just like at Jewell's house, there was no evidence of the spiders at first. The men moved through the entry, scanning for signs of the creatures, but there wasn't even a stray spiderweb. "Which way?" Warren asked, his hand on the spray nozzle, ready to squeeze at a moment's notice.

"Better make it the garage," Rafe said. "It's to the left."

Warren headed that way, finding the door and swinging it open. *This is it,* he thought, unsettled by the darkness. His spine tingled, his palms began to sweat through his tight grip on the sprayer and the flashlight.

He took the first step down and then the next, holding his breath. "Which way?" he whispered.

Rafe followed him down the steps and took the lead, moving around the junk his uncle left behind and over to the workbench. "Sorry, girl, need both hands for this," he said to Boo before setting her on the ground. He shuffled through the scraps, the leftover parts, and all the tools until he finally found what he was looking for.

Rafe held up two large cans of WD-40, grinning. "Found it," he said. He put one of the cans in his pocket for backup, took out the lighter, and nodded to Warren. "To the attic."

Boo followed their footsteps as they headed back into the house and up both sets of stairs. She stood back as her master and Warren shoved their way into the attic, armed to the teeth. Once they were both inside, she followed them through the doorway.

Rafe's hands were sweaty now too, holding the can of WD-40 and the lighter as tight as he was able. They kept slipping in his grip, which only made him sweat harder with the fear that he'd drop them right when he needed them most. "The web was over here," he said, taking the path he remembered around the clutter.

It was still there, spanning clear across the back wall. "It's bigger than I remember," he said.

Warren, still trying to pick his jaw up off the floor, struggled to find words. "I just—I can't believe it," he said.

"I know. Just wait until you see the thing. You'll really shit yourself then."

Warren turned from the web. "You're right. We can't let our guard down yet." The lights from his and Rafe's headlamps were enough to illuminate nearly the entire area around them. There were plenty of shadows to hide still, plenty of furniture and other things to crawl inside, but for the most part, they were able to see clearly.

"It's not here," Rafe said.

"You can't be sure of—"

"Oh yes, I can," Rafe said with certainty. "Trust me. It's not here."

"Okay." Warren took a breath. "Tell me how you know."

"For one, there's not enough room in those shadows to fit the thing. For two, don't you think it would be in its web? And for three, the thing actually *hissed* at me like a cat when it saw the light. Just listen."

They both held their breaths, straining to hear. But they could make out nothing other than Boo panting at their feet and the slight breeze coming from the window that was partially covered in duct tape. Warren pointed at it. "That's how it got in."

"I would imagine it's how it got out, too."

Warren shook his head. He continued to look around the attic. "I keep thinking the thing is going to jump out at me. I can't accept that it's not here. And the littles too. How are they all gone? It doesn't make sense."

"You said yourself that none of this makes any sense. Who the hell knows?" Part of Rafe was glad they were gone. They were prepared to fight, but mentally, he still wasn't sure of the outcome. He never dreamed in a million years that he'd have to go to war with a bunch of insects.

"The littles are working together like a team or a hive mind," Warren said.

"Yeah, and they were working with the big one too —seemed to be trying to protect it or help it out."

Warren ran a hand through his hair. "This is nuts. This is absolutely nuts. Spiders don't do this kind of shit! They don't have a hive mind, they don't eat humans, they don't—"

"Grow eight feet tall?"

"Exactly!" Warren threw up his hands in frustration. "They had to have crawled from the depths of hell —it's the only thing I can think of—wait—" He paused, holding out a hand. There was a memory at the brink of his mind, something important.

They crawled from the depths of hell... they hate the light—not just hate it but fear it... he thought. *Jewell— something about Jewell...* then it hit him. Jewell in the grocery store. She'd cornered him to give him another guilt trip, and he'd tried to ignore her, but something got through.

"The cave. They came from the cave."

Rafe shook his head. "I'm not from around here. I don't know what cave you're talking about."

"The Black Hole cave is an old condemned cave a few miles out of town."

"Nice name."

"I know. But that's where this all started."

"Then I guess that's where we're headed."

Warren eyed Boo in Rafe's arms. "She's going to have to stay out of this."

"She's braver than either of us. She took that beast on without even thinking about it—she saved my life. Where I go, she goes."

Warren pursed his lips. He didn't like the sound of it—one more innocent life to worry about and potentially become a victim before the day was through. She wasn't his though, and he understood he had no right to dictate where she went.

"Fine. I'm driving," he said.

28

A s he drove, Warren watched Rafe from the corner of his eye. The cave wasn't far—less than a twenty-minute drive—but with each mile that passed, he grew more and more concerned. Every few seconds, he'd glance at Rafe and see him scratching at one place or another. At first, he let it pass —everyone scratches themselves—who doesn't have an occasional itch they're not even aware of? But *every* time he looked, he was doing it, and Warren was starting to think it wasn't just a normal itch.

"You have an itch?" he finally asked.

Rafe jumped at the sudden question, breaking the silence between them. "No," he said.

"You keep scratching..."

Rafe looked down at his hands. "I guess I have been. So what? It's nothing."

"You—" Warren cleared his throat. "Listen, I'm not trying to be an ass. I just want to make sure—you didn't get bitten by those things, did you?"

"What? No, of course not. If I did, I would've said something."

"It's just every time I look over there, you're scratching at yourself and it's freaking me the hell out."

"I have dry skin," Rafe said, blushing.

"Dry skin?"

"Yeah." Rafe itched himself again self-consciously.

Warren dropped it. He didn't know what to think, didn't know if maybe Rafe really had been bitten and just didn't know it, but now wasn't the time to turn on each other. He couldn't do this without him and hoped more than anything he was wrong about the scratching.

He tried to push it from his mind, but every few seconds Rafe would reach up in his peripheral vision. The sound of nails scraping against skin filled the space between them. Warren reached for the radio at the same time as Rafe and automatically jerked back so their skin wouldn't touch.

An awkward tension fell between them, and still no music.

FINALLY, after what felt like hours, they pulled up to the parking area outside the cave. "This is it," Warren said.

"Are you ready?" Rafe asked.

"Are you?"

Rafe looked down at Boo in his lap, then back to

Warren. "If something happens to me... will you take care of her?"

"Yeah. Of course I will."

"Thanks," Rafe said. He looked down at his dog, petted her back and scratched behind her ears. "You're braver than me, girl, but I can't let you go inside that cave. I couldn't bear it if something got you in there."

She licked his face in answer.

Rafe nodded to Warren. "She stays in the truck. If I set her down out there, she'll follow us in no matter what I try telling her."

"It's fine by me if she stays here. She'll be safe enough. I'll leave the doors unlocked... just in case." He didn't have to say just in case *what* because that much was clear—just in case *neither* of them made it back out.

Rafe let Boo give him another wet kiss on his face, then said, "Let's go cook some spider."

HE ONLY GAVE in to the urge to look back once. The sight of her leaning her front paws and nose against the window, scratching to be let out with him, cut deep. *Sorry, girl,* Rafe thought, willing her to understand, wishing with everything he had that he was going to make it back out of the cave so he could take care of her. Losing an owner had to be hard on a pet. He knew she'd been close with his uncle. Now if she lost him too —he didn't want that for her.

THEY PUT their headlamps back on, both wearing double. Warren had his sprayer on and ready, along with some backup pesticide for "just in case," and Rafe had the cans of WD-40 and the lighter. They were as ready as they were going to get.

Standing outside the cave entrance, the men shared one last look, a nod, then Rafe started in first. He was only a few feet in when he called, "There's blood."

"I see it," Warren said. Splatter was all over the ground, along with a small pool of it that had dried against the stone.

"Someone was definitely here. Looks like maybe some kids," Rafe said, motioning to the dropped backpack and cell phones smashed near the blood.

They kept going farther in, more wary than ever. Rafe's hands shook, but he held the lighter and can of spray in a firm grip, ready the second he saw even one of the spiders. With all the headlamps they were wearing, the cave was lit up all around them. *If there are spiders in here, they're hiding now*, Rafe thought.

They came out into an enormous open cavern filled with massive boulders of all shapes and jagged icicle-shaped formations rising from the floor and descending from the ceiling. Their lights illuminated colors in the stone, reflecting a rainbow of light back to them. Neither had ever seen such natural beauty before.

"Don't lose focus," Warren said. "Do you see anything?"

"No. Nothing."

They both heard something then—a slight movement in the rocks.

"Do you think we should turn our lights off to lure them out?" Rafe asked.

Warren considered. "We don't know what hell is going to rain down upon us if we do."

"They may stay hidden forever. Just look at this place." Even with the illumination of the headlamps, there were endless dark areas in the cavern—other openings that branched off into seemingly infinite darkness despite the light.

Warren couldn't tell which way the movement came from, but it was unmistakable. There was something in here with them. Doubt began to creep into his mind, whispering, *We're going to die. How the hell are we going to do this with a homemade flamethrower and some pesticide? We're idiots. We're dead-meat idiots. Why didn't we bring the whole town in here with us?*

He shook his head. "Be ready," he said.

Rafe positioned his right thumb over the spark wheel on the lighter and his left over the trigger on the can of WD-40. Then he realized he would have to move one of them to turn off his headlamps and began to worry about which hand would be better to use. Before he could decide, Warren called, "Now!"

Rafe fumbled with both the can and the lighter, dropping the WD-40 at his feet. He managed to grip the lighter but sparked it by mistake and spent precious seconds trying to correct it in his grip.

"What the hell is going on? Turn off your lights," Warren hissed. His were both off.

Rafe bent on his bad leg to pick up the can, almost crying out at the pain. He reached to turn off the back-light, then finally reached for the front.

"Wait!" a voice cried.

Rafe's fingers hovered over the button. "What? What is it?"

"That wasn't me," Warren said.

Both men stood stunned, thinking the same thing —*Who the hell was it?* And, *What now?*

"Who's there?" Rafe called.

There was no answer.

"Am I hearing things?" Rafe asked Warren.

"No. I heard it too."

"Fuck. What do we do?"

"If you don't answer, we're going to turn the light off," Warren called.

"Shh," a muted voice returned.

Rafe and Warren shared another look. There was definitely a third party in here and they were trying to be quiet. Warren winced at how loud they'd been. Whoever this was obviously knew something they didn't, and if they were trying to keep quiet, it was probably for a good reason.

"We need to be quiet," he whispered to Rafe.

Rafe nodded. He reached to turn his second head-lamp back on. When he did, there was a hiss from a few feet away.

His eyes bulged as he turned toward the sound. It was the sound he remembered well—one he would never forget. "That's it," he whispered. "That's the spider."

"This way," Warren said. He took a few steps, reaching to turn one of his headlamps back on too.

There was another louder hiss and more movement. Warren and Rafe shared another look. The spiders were close.

This time, they were able to pinpoint a direction and kept heading that way. Warren reached to turn his second headlamp back on. That's when they saw the web. The one that was huge before—was nothing compared to this—a baby in its shadow.

"It's twice the size of the other one," Rafe breathed. And right in the middle were the bodies. He lost his stomach then, unable to stand the sight of human beings wrapped like insects, waiting to be drained dry by a colossal spider beast.

"There's something moving," Warren hissed. He stepped around Rafe to get a better view of the web.

"Please," a voice croaked. It was the same voice they'd heard before—it was coming from on top of the web and was clearly a young man.

"Where are you?" Warren called.

"You have to be quiet. It's watching."

Warren took a few more steps, allowing the light from his headlamps to shine over the web so he could see. Farther away from the center, one of the bodies was moving slightly—struggling against the sticky substance holding it down. *My god,* Warren thought. *That's where the voice is coming from.*

The young man was the fly in the web, wrapped and

seasoned for the spider to devour at will. Warren could only assume whatever friends he'd come here with—whoever the phones at the entrance belonged to—were up there on the web with him. He turned to Rafe, who was still trying to keep it together. "We have to get him down."

"How the hell are we going to do that?"

"As long as we have light, the spiders will stay away. They haven't come for us yet."

Rafe groaned, bending over again to take more deep breaths. "I know we have to get him down, but I'll be honest, Warren, I'm scared shitless to go up there."

"We'll get them down together. As long as we have the weapons and the lights, we can do this."

Rafe barked a laugh. "*The weapons*? You're hilarious."

Warren shrugged. "Let's go before the spider figures out we're about to steal one of its meals."

29

The problem with a web that size, Warren knew, was that they couldn't just rip it down. The strands were thick and sticky—sticky enough to hold several humans to it as if they were insects. He and Rafe couldn't just climb on top of it either. If they touched it, they'd become stuck—and dinner—too.

"We're going to need fire," Warren said, eyeing the can and lighter in Rafe's hands.

"Don't you think we should save it for, you know— the spiders?" Rafe frowned. The plan was going to hell in a handbasket, and it didn't sit well with him. Yes, they needed to help this person, whoever he was, but they were here for a reason—to kill the damned spiders.

"Yes, you're right, but you also have two cans of it."

"And what happens when it runs out?" Rafe nearly screamed.

"Okay... so we leave him up there? Is that what you're saying? He's a kid, Rafe."

"I'm saying we kill the things *first*. Then, we can take our time and get him down however we need to."

"What if we die? They won't have a chance."

Rafe threw up his hands. "Then we're dead and he's probably dead too."

"Please, you have to stop," the young man on the web said.

Warren spun around. "Don't you want us to save you? We need to figure this—" Rafe's headlamp started flashing behind him. "Stop that," he called, barely holding on to his temper.

"I'm not doing it," Rafe called back.

Warren turned from the web to face him again. His eyes traveled up to the headlamp that Rafe was wearing. That's when the little voice in his mind whispered, *You didn't change the batteries.*

Warren wanted to punch something. He remembered the setting on the headlamps—what it meant when the flashing started.

"By the look on your face, I can tell it's something bad," Rafe said.

Warren ground his teeth. "Your headlamp's batteries are about to die."

Rafe's face drained of what little color was left. "It's okay, right? We have three others..."

The headlamp on the front of Warren's head started flashing.

"No. NO. What are the odds of them dying at the same time? This isn't happening!" Rafe cried.

"We need to get that guy down and go back to the truck. We'll regroup and come back."

Rafe shook his head. "We have the element of surprise *now*. If we leave and come back, they'll be ready for us, and it won't count for shit."

"Listen," Warren said, taking a deep breath. "These are spiders. They're scarier than normal, but they don't *plan,* and they don't *get ready* for anything. They hunt for food, just like any other spiders would."

"I think you're wrong, Warren. And we need to stop wasting time. We need to kill these things and move on with our lives!"

Warren almost laughed. He wanted to say, *Who the hell is the pest guy here?* But instead, he said, "Any minute now—"

He was cut off when there was more movement in the rocks.

"Forget this shit. I'm lighting them up," Rafe cried. His thumb flicked over the lighter, igniting the flame.

A long, low moan came from the guy on the spider web.

A rock fell somewhere in the cave as the spiders moved all around them in the dark.

Rafe's headlamp was no longer flashing but was now dimming lower and lower.

Both of Warren's were flashing now. He started to reach for Rafe, to try and stop him, but he was too slow.

Rafe tapped the front of his dimming headlamp to shut it off, then tapped the back one that hadn't started blinking yet. Then, before Warren could do anything about it, he squeezed the trigger on the can of WD-40, holding it right up next to the lighter's flame. A blast of fire shot out into the darkened cave while a wave of heat singed his eyebrows.

It was more than he'd been expecting. Out of shock, he let go of the trigger, sending them back into a blackness too dark for Warren's pair of flashing headlamps to light. Rafe tried to move forward, but his hurt leg wasn't responding the way he needed. He tripped over himself, falling to the ground hard.

Almost instantly, they came. A swarm of hundreds, moving as a blanket in the dark, eager to cover Rafe in its embrace.

"Turn on the light!" Warren screamed. He moved forward with the sprayer, drenching everything in his path, but it wasn't enough. They kept coming in droves, unfazed by their comrades dying around them.

Rafe pushed his thumb against the lighter's striker wheel. When it didn't light, he did it again and again, on the verge of tears. His mind screamed at him to do twenty things at once—*Stand up! Light the fire! Run! Turn the headlamp back on!* But one idea was louder than all the rest—*Boo is out there waiting.*

The flame came to life.

He squeezed the WD-40, and once again, a torch of fire blew from the can. This time, Rafe found success. All around him, the spiders squealed and hissed in pain as they burned. The ones already covered in the pesticide had it the worst, popping and exploding like burned popcorn.

Rafe kept the trigger squeezed until the can ran out. He climbed to his feet. "How are we doing?" he cried.

Warren shook his head in the dark. "Plenty left. For now. You have the other can?"

Rafe dropped the empty can to reach in his pocket for the spare. For a moment, his heart stopped. He couldn't feel it. *It fell out. We're going to die. It's all over. We're going to be eaten by fucking spiders!* he thought, then his fingers brushed the can, and he could've screamed his relief.

They both heard the spiders regrouping and moving again. They had moments before they'd have to fight again. But would they have enough to fight with? And what would they do when the big one came? They both had the same concerns, but neither spoke them.

"Yeah, I got it," Rafe said. "Can't walk worth a goddamn, though."

"You don't need to walk. They'll come to you."

Warren's lights both went out, leaving them in total darkness.

The person on the web made another sound, then there was a crunching sound. Both Warren and Rafe realized it was too late to save him. The spider had been on the web all along—waiting, just like they were warned.

"He tried to tell us," Warren said.

"Fuck," Rafe said, on the verge of losing his stomach again. He vowed to save the other can for the mammoth. He wouldn't waste it on the littles—*let Warren spray the shit out of them*, he thought. He knew it would be hard, not just because he wanted to kill all of them but because of the lack of light. The fire was a beacon of survival—without it, they were in an abyss of darkness.

"Here they come," Warren called. He not only heard them but could also feel them moving all around. There was a shift in the air, and he knew the big one was here too, hiding somewhere in the darkness. "Come on, you big bitch, come on!" he cried.

Rafe reached to turn his front headlamp back on. The light was dim, barely registering against the sheet of black he was faced with, but at least he could see his own feet with it. When he saw what was stepping toward him, he almost wanted to turn it back off so he'd not have to look at it. "Warren," Rafe choked.

"What's wrong?"

"There's more than one."

The remaining light, though fading and dull, was enough to show the silhouette of the giant spider Rafe had seen in his attic—the one he'd believed was a mammoth. But beside it now was another, nearly twice its size. It was gargantuan by comparison—so massive that they both had to crane their necks to look up at its head.

"It's the female," Warren breathed.

"Is it looking at us? I can't see. It's too dark."

"You can assume she is," Warren said. A calmness washed over him with the reality that they didn't stand a chance against this being. They were ants playing with fire against a creature nearly the size of a house. It would take more than some bug spray and a little fire to kill it. It would take a bomb, a—

Warren turned to Rafe. "We need to make an explosion. It's the only way we make it out of here. Maybe we don't kill them all, but we block them in so they can't get into the world again."

"I'm game. How the hell do we do it?"

The last of the light went out, along with any semblance of safety it provided.

"Follow me!" Warren yelled.

"I can't see!"

"I can't either, just move!"

Rafe moved in the direction he believed Warren to be. Sweat was pouring out of every orifice of his skin. His leg was killing him every time he put pressure on it, but he wasn't going to let it slow him down. He'd rather lose the thing altogether than be forced to become spider food.

He stumbled along after Warren, aware that he was lagging behind. He reached to scratch his head and thought, *Jesus, this thing is itchy as hell.* He ripped the dead headlamp from his forehead, threw it behind him, hoping he'd hit something, then realized he still had another strap attached to him. In that moment, he wanted to slap himself silly. There was the second light he'd forgotten all about.

Rafe tapped the second light that was still good, swiveled it around so it was facing forward, and backpedaled as the female spider was about to pin him to the floor. With a speed he didn't know he possessed, he ignited the lighter while squeezing the can of WD-40 and lit the spider's leg on fire. His ears rang with the screeching, but he managed to dodge out of the way when the male spider advanced on him.

Warren screamed from ahead, "Come on, almost there!"

"I'm trying!" Rafe cried. He used the makeshift blowtorch to singe the giant's legs. It was enough to buy him a few feet of cover—enough to catch back up with Warren.

"They're on my ass," Rafe said.

"Good," Warren said. He held up his spare pesticide container. "This is pressurized. We're going to use the lighter to make a big boom and hopefully, it'll close the cave in. Problem solved."

"Let's hope it's that easy," Rafe said. He wanted nothing more than to be outside in the truck with his dog, driving a thousand miles away to safety. He'd take her somewhere warm for a vacation, maybe spend Christmas on the beach together. Forget redoing the house, forget everything.

They were close to the entrance now, where the opening was narrow, and an explosion would be effective. The giants were having a hard time getting to them, but they were still spiders and somehow found a way to wrap themselves up smaller to fit through where they wanted to be. Rafe watched in horror at how small a space they could squeeze into.

"Give me the lighter and the can," Warren said, setting his equipment down.

Rafe handed them over.

"Now, get the hell out of here."

"What?"

"One of us has to light it. How else is it going to happen?"

Rafe shook his head. "No. No. I thought—"

Warren looked back at the opening where they were approaching. The spiders were squeezing through, almost on top of them now, the littles leading the charge. There was no more time to argue, no more time to talk. He shoved Rafe. "I'll be right behind you. Run, goddammit!"

Rafe gripped Warren's arm, knowing full well this was it. Warren wasn't going to follow. He was the pest guy, and he was doing what he did best—exterminating unwanted pests. Rafe nodded. Then he ran as fast as his battered leg would allow.

WARREN GAVE Rafe as much time as he could to get out, but when the first of the spiders were just through the narrow opening, he knew his time was up. *Please let this work*, he thought. He lit the lighter.

RAFE SCREAMED as the blast knocked him flat just outside the cave entrance. The plan worked. The blast was enough to seal the opening closed—not even the smallest of the spiders would find a crack to get through. "You did it, Warren," Rafe said.

Guilt swelled in his chest. He tried not to tell himself that it should've been him down there igniting the fire or that he should've spent less time arguing about saving the kid on the web and just went along with what the pest guy was saying. He stood to make his way to his dog.

She was in the same spot, standing with her front paws against the window, waiting for him. She barked when he smiled and waved at her. Rafe closed his eyes as she licked his face.

"Let's go, girl," he said.

He reached for the ignition—the keys weren't there. They were back in the cave, in Warren's pocket.

PART VIII

30

The Hamilton family, who fled their land and home, along with most of their worldly possessions, continued running as far as they could from Rock Creek—away from the spiders. Hart clamped his eyes shut as he tossed and turned in his seat while his wife drove the truck. Sweat was pouring out of him, but he hardly noticed. The only thing on his mind was the pain in his lower belly.

"Maybe we should find a hospital," Ivey said, not for the first time.

"No. I'm not going to the damned hospital for an upset stomach. Are you kidding me? How many times are you going to make me say it?"

"Honey, you keep saying that, but you've been getting steadily worse since we left Rock Creek. We've been driving for over fourteen hours, almost nonstop. I'm tired, Hart."

"I can drive again!" Kala chimed in from the back.

Hart ground his teeth against another wave of pain.

He was beginning to feel nauseous now, and felt a fever starting, which didn't help anything. "No," he ground out.

"But you let me before!"

"That was only when there were no other cars," Ivey said. "You don't even have your license, Kala."

"Why should that matter? You're too tired to drive, and Dad can't. I'm the only one left if we have to keep going."

"We're going to stop as soon as we get to the next town," Ivey said. "A thousand miles is enough distance. Nothing is going to get us out in the middle of nowhere, Montana." She checked the kids in the rearview mirror. "Xander, how are you doing?"

"I'm okay," he said, his eyes never moving from his tablet.

Ivey placed a hand on her husband's arm. "Just hang in there, Hart. We'll stop at the next drugstore." She frowned. "There has to be one coming up soon. There's been nothing for miles."

Hart jerked in his seat. He twisted and clutched at his abdomen, desperate to put counter tension against the burning agony. He was so focused on making it stop, on surviving through it, that he hardly registered what she was saying. *It's fine. Everything is fine. You ate some bad fish, and everyone knows that shit will mess you up like no other,* he thought, trying to calm himself down. *Think about the land. Think about the house we're going to build. Think about—*

A pressure was building inside. Hart stopped moving. "Pull over," he said.

"What?" Ivey asked, not sure she heard right.

"Pull over! Pull over!" Hart clamped his legs together and squeezed down on the muscles in his rear end. *No, no, not going to shit yourself today, sir*, he thought, willing his wife to slam on the brakes so he could get out. He couldn't bear for the kids to see him like this, it was bad enough already.

Luckily, Ivey got the message loud and clear. The truck jerked to a stop on the side of the highway. Hart climbed out before the wheels could completely still. A few feet away, he dropped his pants behind a bush, where he lost his insides.

As he squatted, hoping and praying that his family couldn't see him, a great gush left his body. Chunky midnight-black liquid pooled at his feet, reeking of shit, death, and his own decay. Hart was so consumed with breathing through the contractions that he didn't notice at first what was in the waste being extracted from his bowels.

"Mom, can we *please* roll up the window? I can smell it from here," Xander said.

Ivey rolled up the window where Hart had been sitting.

"How long is he going to be?" Kala asked. "He's been out there at least twenty minutes already. Are we just going to sit here all—"

"Stop it, Kala. You know he's sick."

"But you complain about it all the time!"

"Yeah, well, that's me. Not you."

"This is so stupid."

Ivey opened her door. "I'm going to check on Dad. Both of you stay here." She met Kala's eyes. "*Please*."

The minute she was out, she had to cover her nose with her shirt. Xander was right. Whatever was coming out of Hart stank like hell. *Such a stubborn fool for not letting me take him to the doctor*, she thought.

"Hart, are you okay?" she called, taking a few steps toward him.

He mumbled something unintelligible.

"I can't hear you," she said, coming closer to the bush he was behind. Ivey waited for him to tell her to go away—it was such a personal thing, and he was normally sensitive about it when he got sick like this, but he wasn't saying anything to her now other than moaning in pain. She was growing more worried by the second.

Something isn't right with him, she thought. Past the point of concern over modesty, she stepped around the bush to see him.

Hart was kneeling, knees spread, bent far over, so the top of his head was touching the ground. Ivey's eyebrows narrowed at first, confused at his position and his missing pants—but then she saw what was coming out of him.

Spiders. The small ones she'd seen before—but there were more than just those. Massive black legs were *peeling* him apart, birthing themselves from his anus. Hart's body racked in pain and contraction after contraction as his intestine tried to rid itself of the foreign parasite.

Ivey was rooted to her spot, watching in horror as her husband writhed in agony, as the spiders crawled out from inside him—covered in his blood and fluids. That this was real, this was actually happening, hovered just outside her conscious mind. She shook her head, unable to comprehend what was happening.

More long black legs came out from Hart's body. They pulled and gripped and dug into his flesh. His skin and muscle tore open. And finally, the spider was free.

Ivey stared at the *thing* bigger than she was—bigger than Hart. She inhaled, ready to scream at the top of her lungs, but the thing was fast. A pair of fangs sank into her chest, robbing the breath from her lungs. The scream died on her lips as she was pumped full of venom, destined to meet the same fate as her husband.

KALA WATCHED her mom cover her nose as she walked from the car. *That's right,* she thought, satisfied by her mom's discomfort. She was a hypocrite to complain and not let her say her piece and deserved to be just as uncomfortable as the rest of them. *I hope Dad shits on you,* she thought as her mom walked into the distance.

She brought out the novel she'd been reading during the trip and continued where she'd left off. The words swept her away into a whole new world. The characters had their own, far more interesting lives, with none of the problems that she had. They were smart and witty and always seemed to make her forget her own reality.

Eventually, she looked up from the book to realize she'd nearly finished it. Her brows furrowed. "Xander, what time is it?"

"I dunno. Why?"

"You have it right there on your screen."

"I'm playing a game."

She took a breath. Out the window, the sun was fading into twilight. "Something isn't right with Mom and Dad. They've been gone way too long."

Xander shrugged.

"Listen to me." She put both hands against his cheeks to force his eye contact. "I'm going to check on them. You need to pay attention."

"Why does it matter anyway? He's just pooping."

"Do you even realize what you're saying? It doesn't take *hours* to poop! And where's Mom?"

"Okay, this is Dad we're talking about."

"I don't care. It doesn't even take *him* that long."

Xander considered, then nodded. "Okay." He locked his tablet and set it on the seat between them. "What do you want me to do?"

"Just watch out the window, and if something happens, go for help."

He frowned. "I don't know how to drive. Maybe I should—"

"No. I'm going to do it," she said. She sighed. "I'm sure they're just out there talking or something anyway. Just stay here and watch, okay?"

He nodded.

Kala climbed out of the back seat, slamming the

door behind her. The smell hit her like a blast, gagging her and bringing tears to her eyes. She covered her nose and mouth with her shirt, the way her mom had done. "Mom?" she cried through the fabric. "Dad?"

No answer came.

Thinking they couldn't hear, she brought the shirt back down off her nose and mouth to try again. "Mom? Dad?"

Nothing.

"What the hell, you guys?" *That should get a rise out of them,* she thought. They hated when she used foul language.

But neither of her parents said a word to challenge her.

A sliver of fear ran through Kala. It wasn't just worry at this point—she *knew* with certainty that there was something wrong. What she couldn't decide was if she should approach the way her mom did or stay back with Xander in the truck. *I can leave to go find help.* Xander couldn't drive, but she could. *But what would I say? My parents are behind a bush and won't come out?* she scolded herself.

The need to know was too strong. Besides, her subconscious was right: if she was going to get help, she had to know what the problem was in the first place. *Maybe Dad shit his brains out and Mom passed out from the nasty smell*, she thought with a smile, almost laughing at the ridiculous paths her mind traveled.

Kala walked toward the bush. "I can't believe you guys are making me come over there," she said, using the tone her dad always likes to use.

She came around the other side—and stopped

dead in her tracks. Her hands flew to her mouth as a gasp escaped her lips. Tears sprang to her eyes and rolled down her cheeks.

They were both dead.

Blood and gore and feces were everywhere. Her dad's entire body was broken open mush, the only thing that remained halfway recognizable was part of his face. Tiny black spiders—the ones Asia had been so afraid of when she banged on their RV door—were crawling all over him, nesting inside his flesh, eating it, and doing God knows what else.

Her mom was not much better off. She wasn't cracked open, but Kala was sure her insides were still mush. She was wrapped in a spider web, attached to a larger web, and a giant spider was sucking her insides out through her mouth.

Kala choked. Hot tears rolled down her cheeks. She backed away slowly in an effort not to attract the giant's attention. She didn't account for all the eyes, though.

Kala saw the moment it noticed her. She ran for the car, screaming at the top of her lungs for Xander to open the door.

XANDER WATCHED through the window as his sister had asked. He didn't think it was necessary, as she did, until he saw what was chasing her. His jaw dropped, watching the massive arachnid reaching its hairy black legs out toward her, baring its fangs, like it wanted to *eat* her.

"Oh my—"

Kala slammed into the car door, staring through the window at Xander with wild eyes. She was screaming something, but he couldn't make out what she was saying. He tilted his head at her, trying to read her lips through the glass. "Why are you out there yelling?" he asked. He looked to the front seats. *Where's Mom and Dad?* he thought.

Kala scratched into the paint, fumbling for the door handle, yanking, yanking—

"It's locked," Xander said, calm as if he was telling her a simple fact.

"Open it!" she screamed through her tears.

Xander started to reach forward, but his seat belt held him back. He sat back down, then reached to unfasten it.

"Hurry up!" Kala cried.

Having no sense of urgency whatsoever, Xander let the seat belt fall off his shoulder, then looked back up toward his sister through the window. She was no longer screaming—that was a relief. He hated when she screamed at him.

She pulled away from the window almost in slow motion—and that's when Xander saw the spider again. Its coal-black eyes pierced into him as if to promise *you're next*. Like magic, the shock faded. Xander realized the exact situation he was in, and what had just happened to his entire family.

"I can't drive," he whispered, his chin wobbling. He eyed the keys still in the ignition. Out the window, the spider was dragging Kala away now. *This is the only chance I'm going to get*, he thought.

With shaking hands, Xander crawled over the center console into the driver's seat. He reached for the brake pedal as he'd seen his parents do—but he couldn't reach it, so he moved the seat forward as far as he could. He twisted the key in the ignition. D *is for drive*, he thought, as he moved the shifter into position.

Xander gave the spider one final look before he pressed his foot on the accelerator, leaving his family far behind.

31

The Rock Creek sheriff received a strange call that night from another sheriff in a small Montana town. "I have a boy here who's giving me the craziest story I've ever heard," the Montana sheriff said.

"For some reason, that doesn't surprise me. I've had a hell of a last few days—all kinds of strange reports that don't make any sense."

"I'm sure I have them all beat with this one," the Montana sheriff said.

"Try me."

"Well... this boy says his entire family was eaten by a giant spider while they were pulled off the highway for his dad to take a shit. He thinks the spider was inside his dad—*pooped him out,* he says."

"And the family is from Rock Creek, I take it?"

"That's right. My deputy pulled him over when he about ran into a telephone pole. He knew there was something going on when he saw he wasn't even ten years old. And there's more."

"I'm listening."

"The kid says he and his family ran from home when a girl died inside their bathroom. He said she was eaten by the spiders too."

"Good god."

"Yeah. Tell me."

"Did he give you their address?"

"He did. But, sheriff—he about had a fit when he gave it to me. He made me swear that I would warn you to not go at night or, if you do, bring lights. He says the spiders don't like the light."

The Rock Creek sheriff sighed. "Poor kid. You can tell him not to worry. We'll bring plenty of light with us."

RAFE and his dog were still on foot, weaving their way through the forest as they tried to find civilization. "Shouldn't be much farther, girl," he said to Boo, faithfully by his side.

The muffled traffic from through the trees told him the highway wasn't far. They kept going, slowly but surely. Eventually Rafe picked Boo up and carried her for a ways so she could have a break. He wished there was someone to pick him up too—his leg was in bad shape, only getting worse and slowing him down.

They came to the highway, but there were no

drivers who wanted to stop. Rafe didn't blame them. In this day and age, who knew the kind of person you'd be picking up, especially one limping along with a dog in his arms.

A sheriff pulled onto the shoulder just ahead of them.

"Well that's just great," Rafe said. He knew he needed to tell the police about Warren and the cave and his handyman in his attic—if his body was still there—but he wasn't sure *how* exactly to do all that yet. There was a fine line and if he crossed it, he'd be seen as a lunatic.

"Where you headed?" the sheriff called out his window.

"Over off Golden Road," Rafe said.

"I normally wouldn't do this, but since I'm headed to that exact road as it is—you want a lift?"

"I appreciate it," Rafe said. He got into the back of the cruiser with Boo, deciding to keep his information to himself for now. He'd figure out the story first—it had to be a good one—then he'd make his report.

THE SHERIFF GOT on his radio to alert his deputies he was making a detour. He was too preoccupied with the story he'd heard on the phone to bother with the traveler in his back seat. The man was lucky. Any other day, the sheriff would've been curious about what he was doing on the side of the highway with a little dog, limping along like that, looking like he'd been beaten.

But the sheriff was off his game and out of sorts. Things had been going on in the town of Rock Creek. All these reports, all the fear of spiders going around— who the hell wasn't afraid of them anyway? But all these reports and complaints. What went on at the hospital and then the town supermarket—he knew poor Warren had business up to his eyeballs lately. And now this ugly story with the boy and his family—

The radio crackled as a deputy called in. "Sheriff, you're gonna want to get down here ASAP. It looks like that story you heard might not be so far-fetched after all."

The sheriff grabbed the mic. "What the hell are you talking about?"

"There are spiders everywhere in here. We can't even get inside without them crawling all over every- one. It's like there's a nest or something," the deputy said.

Fear began to work its way down Rafe's spine with every word he heard through the radio. "Sheriff," he said. "I have a story I think you're going to want to hear."

SEVEN HUNDRED MILES away from Rock Creek, in the middle of a desolate highway in Montana, a female spider was laying her eggs. She was of an ancient breed from a time when her kind ruled. They were not seen as giant beasts but instead, as queens and kings, worshipped and feared as gods.

Her host had served as a fine meal today, along with the others he'd brought with him. She had plenty of meat to fill her belly and plenty more left when her offspring hatched. The littles would spread out across the land to find a new place for shelter as she grew, a place to hide her from the light and to lure new meat as they multiplied—until the time came when they were plenty enough to become gods once again.

<u>DON'T MISS BOOK 2:</u>
<u>INFESTATION</u>

Currently being serialized on Kindle Vella.
More information available at:
https://www.klucasauthor.com/infestation

Man-eating spiders have infested the town of Rock
Creek. The entrance to Black Hole Cave has been
sealed with the deadly spiders inside, but there are
more lurking in the shadows...and inside the residents.
With bodies stacking and danger lurking around every
corner, townsfolk are desperate to find a solution
before they all become the next meal.

THANK YOU

THANK YOU FOR READING!

Enjoyed Arachnophobia?

Please consider leaving a review.

Reviews help authors more than you might think. Even just a few words make a difference and are greatly appreciated. The best place to review is whichever retailer you purchased from, but you can also consider Goodreads or BookBub.

ACKNOWLEDGMENTS

First and foremost, I'd like to thank my husband and son for being my biggest fans, for all the support, encouragement, and understanding, and for traveling this journey by my side no matter how crazy the road gets. I love you to infinity and beyond!

Thank you to my editing team at My Brother's Editor for being so amazing at what you do and so flexible when I'm running behind.

I'd also like to thank Sara for being the first to read this book and give me helpful feedback, and an even bigger thank you for all of your support and encouragement from the very first book of mine that you came across.

Also, a special thank you to my Patreon subscribers, especially Justin. Your support and interest in my work means the world!

To my faithful readers, you and your continued support are everything to me! Thank you for sticking with me, for encouraging me, fanning the flames, and for picking up each new book that releases.

And finally, thank you, dear reader, for showing me

your support by reading this book. Whether you are new to my work or are one who keeps coming back for more, I truly hope you enjoyed the read.

ABOUT
K. LUCAS

K. Lucas is an author who lives for the unexpected twist. Originally from California, she now lives in the Pacific Northwest with her husband, son, dogs, cats, and chickens. After earning a bachelor's degree in information technology, she became a homeschool mom and then a full-time author. She loves all things thrilling & chilling, and her favorite pastimes include reading, watching scary movies, and exploring nature.

www.klucasauthor.com

CONNECT WITH
K. LUCAS

To subscribe for text message updates
text KLUCAS to 833-259-1871

See K. Lucas's website for more info, signed copies, and
to sign up for newsletter updates!

Website:
www.klucasauthor.com
Newsletter:
www.klucasauthor.com/newslettersignup

patreon.com/klucas

amazon.com/author/klucas

goodreads.com/klucas

bookbub.com/authors/k-lucas

instagram.com/author_klucas

facebook.com/author.klucas

tiktok.com/@klucasauthor

pinterest.com/klucasauthor

twitter.com/AuthorKLucas

ALSO BY
K. LUCAS

Made in United States
North Haven, CT
22 June 2024

53887485R00150